His Christmas Bunny

BY BILLIE JADE KERMACK

Special thanks go out to the amazing Author Annie Charme, my Pun-Queen who also writes brilliant romance novels. Check out her stuff. This book wouldn't have been ready in time for a Christmas release without her guidance and support, I am eternally grateful.

To the formidable duo Dusty Shirley and Jenn Maryk, I feel very lucky to have you ladies on my team, you always have my back and I am forever in awe of how you can bring a team of readers together with such finesse. You ladies light up my heart and rock my soul.
To my ARC team - some are new to my work, some are seasoned to the emotional rollercoasters I take you on. I really hope you enjoy this one and thank you for agreeing to take time out of your lives to read Mia and Logan's story. I appreciate every single one of you more than you know.

Readers Note

"His Christmas Bunny" is a sweet and spicy festive novella. It's a fun filled short read. All of my romances promise hot book boyfriends with cinnamon roll sweet personalities, tattoos and dirty intentions and this one is no exception.

To family and friends, thank you for your support in my journey so far, but this is your warning, there will be graphic sex and a fuck-tonne of foul language from this point on, so feel free not to read any further if it might make Christmas gatherings awkward for you. You also may or may not pick up an Easter bunny Kink, I will not apologise for that one, life is meant to be filled with the weird and the wonderful...

Playlist

Eartha Kitt - Santa Baby

Creep - Radiohead

Jingle Bell Rock - Bobby Helms

Baby it's cold outside - Tom Jones & Cerys Matthews

The Summoning - Sleep Token

The night we met - Lord Huron

All I want for Christmas is you - Mariah Carey

Last Christmas - Wham

Underneath the tree - Kelly Clarkson

Happy Christmas - John Lennon & Yoko Ono

Hallelujah - Pentatonix

Fairytale of New York - The Pogues & Kirsty MacColl

Santa Claus is coming to town - The Jackson 5

Merry Christmas Everyone - Shakin' Stevens

Blue Christmas - Elvis Presley

Please come home for Christmas - The Eagles

She hates me - Puddle Of Mudd

Man with the bag - Jessie J'

For all those channeling their inner

Hoe, Hoe, Hoe.

The ones that would happily be

devoured whilst tied down with tinsel...

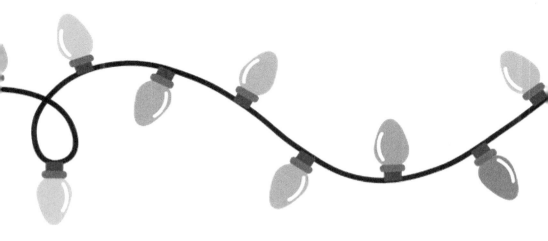

CHAPTER One

MIA

There is something to be said for people who make epically shit life choices on a regular basis, I'm allowed to have an opinion on the matter because I seem to fail constantly when faced with the simplest of decisions. Take this evening for example. A normal human being would have worn the sluttiest outfit to this costume party, it is after all a gathering that people excitedly mark off in their calendars as being the must attend event of the year. It's always lavish and promises a good time with enough food and booze to keep everyone in attendance going for a week if Logan saw fit to extend the celebrations. I sometimes think the birthday boy, or birthday man I should say, only invites me each year to see what idiotic costume his little sister's nerdy best friend will wear. Being the butt of someone's joke isn't a new fit for me, I'm a seasoned traveller on the *'how can Mia fuck up today'* train. Do I follow the grain and do what every other girl in here has done, and take advantage of the fact that I can be whoever I want to be tonight? No, I, Mia Jane Grayson,

moronically decided funny and unexpected would be my go-to descriptors for tonight's event. I might as well slap a loser.

stamp to my forehead and be done with the awkward formalities of people trying not to stare.

'I should go home,' I whine, wearing more than anyone else in here but feeling too exposed as everyone in attendance side eyes me. They are laughing and gossiping as I try to hide behind a pink and gold balloon display, that really does nothing but enhance my costume choice. I flick my coiled lengths of deep red hair over my shoulder with a huff, wishing I was at home wearing sweatpants and an oversized band tee, the only part of that ensemble that would be fluffy would be the neon orange socks I would pair it with.

'If you go home, I go home,' Candice utters distinctly, but I can hear the edge of disappointment lingering in her tone, I'd be gutted if I was the reason she had to leave. 'The pink in your outfit makes the blue of your eyes pop,' she offers the compliment up with a shrug of her shoulders, it's a poor attempt to placate me, but I love her for the effort.

Usually, I don't much care what people think of me. I'm the first one to rejoice when I don't fit into the crowd, but this is different, this isn't just any party, this is *his* birthday party. I glance around the room but he's nowhere to be seen.

'It's okay to admit you have a thing for my brother,' Candice chuckles, reading me like a book as she sways along to *Radioheads Creep*, her Ann Summers sailor outfit cinched in at all the right places to enhance her curvy figure. If my cheeks weren't already rosy with embarrassment at her mention of me having *a thing* for Logan, I would be flushing with a different kind of heat, of the pussy clenching variety, because she's not wrong. He's brutish, older than me and probably slept with most of the women in here, or at least that is what I've heard, but I can't deny there is something about Logan Sinclair. If he wasn't already repulsed by the mere thought of his little sister's best friend mooning over him, this outfit would be the final nail in the coffin at the idea of anything happening between us. I tug off the black nose with the whiskers attached, finally able to suck down a full breath and use my newfound ability to fill my lungs only to *harrumph* sadly.

The Marquee set up in the private gardens of Wenthorp Manor is massive, pink and gold silk drapery wound with fairy lights hanging from the ceiling, a large net filled with balloons of the same colours secured high above the dance floor. The makeshift bar is along one wall of the white linen enclosure, a hotdog stand and a kebab table flanking on the opposite side. I'm too wired to eat or drink anything just yet.

'You look cute,' Candice lies again as she runs a manicured finger up the bushy rabbit ears propped up on my head.

'Best friends don't bullshit.' I press through clenched lips, our one rule to stick by. Well that and never trusting food served at three AM from a cart in the middle of Piccadilly Circus, our go-to after a bar hop bender.

'Look he might not even turn up.' She coos, taking a bite out of her second mustard smothered hotdog, the copious amounts of onion topping hiding the sausage completely. Good luck to Randy when he tries smooching her later.

'Of course he will turn up. It's his freaking party Candice. You are too free and easy with the bullshit tonight.' I bark at her, zero bite in my tone because I know she's only trying to make me feel better. It doesn't work but it could be worse, I could be wearing a full-on furry rabbit bodysuit you'd usually find in a shopping centre somewhere at Easter.

'Who's the one bullshitting now?' That little inner voice snaps as I catch sight of my reflection in the mirrored punch bowl. There is no confusion about what costume I have committed to.

'Ladies,' I recognise immediately the gruff tone of the man standing behind us. I tap my converse clad foot against the floor in the hopes that it will open up and swallow me whole, but sadly no such luck.

My stomach plummets south and my heart constricts in my chest as I turn to face the man of the hour, the birthday boy that has a chorus of pretty young women dressed in Playboy bunny outfits flanking either side of him. If anyone ever tells you sexiness is subjective, they are fools, there is no grey area on what costumes are the more alluring as the women pepper me with pitiful glances. Logan is the epitome of tall, dark and handsome and fuck me if it doesn't screw with my head every time we are this close to one another. The women that look more like models than college students surrounding Logan clearly agree with me, as they move to drape themselves over his broad muscled body like they are fine pieces of expensive jewellery, I note the one playing with the cropped black hair at the nape of his neck is eyeing me like I'm a piece of dirt on the heel of one of her seriously high stilettos. At twenty-three Logan is four-years-older than me, the fact that I have been in love with him all these years is completely beside the point, because I have zero claim over him. He has always been out of my league and right now I want to run home and crawl into bed with a pint of ice cream to watch *Vampire diary* re-runs, wallowing in self-pity while I allow myself to daydream about an alternative reality where he could maybe be mine.

The DJ spins a new beat, and the women disperse, hollering and cheering as they clamour to the dance floor like a flock of majestic flamingos.

'Having fun Bunny?' Logan steps into my space and I swear he can hear the cavernous thump of my ragged heart, as it fights to break free of my chest, even with the pulse of the thrashing rock music in the background. He shouldn't be able to affect me the way that he does. At six-foot-four, with tanned skin, cropped black hair and built with muscles from playing sports, Logan is an exquisite example of look but don't touch.

'Don't call me that, Soldier boy,' I bite back as he takes in my costume, his amused gaze travelling up from my oversized bunny feet to the tippety-top of my long bunny ears. When his muddy green eyes track back down and lock with mine, I swallow back the gasp that is lingering on my tongue. There's too much unspoken emotion lingering behind his tight expression. Two lines of war paint don either cheek and his smile broadens as he puffs out his chest, clearly enjoying my reaction to the perusal of his body. The tight black vest looks near to bursting at the seams, his tattooed arms adding an element of danger to his already mouthwatering look. I chance a glance lower, past the fake dog-tags around his neck that will soon be replaced with a real set once he's deployed, to his khaki cargo pants, numerous pockets filled with little glass bottles of *Jim Beam* that he's likely been handing out to his guests like miniature party favours run down both legs. His military belt holds a prop gun, a plastic baton and what appears to be a pair of very authentic chrome handcuffs. I push away the imagery of him using those on me before my face goes bright pink to match my costume.

'GI Joe again, some would say three years in a row is two years too many.' I snap, masking the neediness in my tortured tone.

'And *some* would say why mess with perfection,' he chortles, sliding his prop gun out of his belt and levelling it under my chin, tipping my head back to meet his gaze. 'Which *some* would you be Bunny?' he growls, low enough that only I can hear him, he's too close, I'm sure he can smell the desperation rolling off me in waves.

'Hit me brother,' Tate, the rugby teams full back dressed as *Hulk Hogan,* roars as he slaps Logan on the back interrupting our exchange, dropping into tackling prep position and opening his mouth. Logan turns and places the barrel of the gun on his lower lip and squirts a clear liquid into his mouth. Tate is gone as quick as he arrived, tackling another member of the team on route to the bar.

'Becky,' Candice squeals, pulling my attention away from her brother. I'd almost forgotten she was even behind me, so transfixed with the caged bubble of existence Logan seems to pull me into whenever he is in my orbit. Candice totters across the room to our friend as she stumbles into the party halfcocked, likely with a spiked blood level to rival any noted member of the infamous 27 club that had alcohol as their preferred drug of choice. Becky's middle name should

11

be *party hard.* The first one to arrive and the last to leave any celebration, Becky was referred to often as hardcore to the extreme. It's only eight PM and she already has her fingers wound around the straps of her heels in her hand. I can't quite make out the costume she has on, but the tight fitted red lace bodice puts her in the same category as every other woman but me right now. She looks sexy, even while inebriated with her lipstick smeared around her chin.

'You look cute Bunny,' Logan dips and whispers into my ear as though he knows I am mentally comparing myself to the other women in attendance. The barely there presence of his lips against my throat causes a zing of electricity to whizz up my spine. I don't tell him off for using the nickname this time, if I'm honest I quite like the husky way it sounds as his warm whiskey laced breath hits my cheek. I fight the urge to reach up and trace my fingers across the scar that makes a path through one of his eyebrows, that little one-of-a-kind mark flooding me with an onslaught of memories I'm not in the right frame of mind to address right now. 'Save me a dance,' he chuckles and for a moment I wonder if I imagined the words, before he slinks off into the crowd, gifting me one of those megawatt smiles of his, before dancing bodies swallow him up and he disappears. I clench my thighs, willing the thrum of excitement that has my knickers soaked to relax. It doesn't work and if the cheeky glint in Logan's eyes were an indicator, he was certainly aware of the effect he was having on me. Why can't I think straight with him around?

'What the hell baby?' Strong arms loop around my furry waist and I'm tugged back against a large body. I silently note my flash of frustration at the fact that it isn't the man I had secretly hoped it would be, because that's just plain awful. Trevor and I have been dating for two months now, we attend the same philosophy lectures and have enough in common to keep the conversation flowing. He's a little hot and heavy sometimes but for the most part, he is..... My train of thought is interrupted when I mentally search for the word, but when the only one that comes to mind is nice, my shoulders slump and I plaster a smile on my face.

Will it ever get easier, will I ever see another guy in the same light that I do Logan?

The faint laughter of my little inner voice hits me hard, and I spin in Trevor's arms as he eyes my costume with confused interest.

'You don't like it?' I coo, swaying my hips, my feet rooted to the spot, the smile that was at first forced easing a little at the edges as he beams down at me, his shoulder length blond hair pulled back into a bun at the nape of his neck, a crystal encrusted eyepatch over one eye and a wide brimmed pirate hat pulled down onto his head.

'I love it,' he grins, and I relax a little more, the tension caused by Logan's mere presence seeping out of my limbs. I take the red solo cup from Trevor's hand and knock back whatever alcohol he has in there, Bourbon, I think.

'I would love it even more if it was on my bedroom floor.' He lulls suggestively, running his finger across my cheek and down to my lips.

Trevor and I haven't exactly got that far in our relationship yet and while he tries to hide his frustrations, they are becoming harder to mask, the alcohol isn't helping any when a fleeting scowl pinches between his brows when I pull away from him a fraction. I'm just not ready yet. He knows it, I know it, fuck if my choice in costume wasn't enough of a flashing warning light, it's clear I have no idea what it entails to be a sexual being. Mia the virgin, Mia the prude, Mia the cocktease…. I've heard it all.

As though he has connected with me through the power of telekinesis, I feel Logan's disapproving glare from across the room as he stares our way before I've even had a chance to turn my head to seek him out.

Trevor is probably Logan's least favourite person, and he's warned me once or twice about my decision to date him. With them both playing the fly-half positions on opposing Rugby teams they are used to getting into some heated scraps, on and off the pitch. In my defence, I hadn't known about the trouble brewing between them when Trevor had approached me in the on-campus coffee shack and insisted I was way too pretty to be buying my own mocha latte.

I break my stare off with Logan, tamping down the fluttering that is whipping about low in my belly, a noted side effect of being trapped under his steely perusal. Trevor is dragged away by a fellow teammate towards the snooker table set up with a game of beer pong. I wave him off because if I'm honest, I'm grateful for the respite, dodging his advances is becoming a full-time job. I should want to sleep with my *nice* boyfriend. Why is this so damn hard?

Deciding I don't have the answer to that particular question I refill my cup with a ladle of spiked punch and relish the burn in my throat as I swallow it back. I am far too coherent right now. Pushing my bunny ears back in place, I suck down a confident breath that fills my lungs to near bursting and go in search of Candice and Randy. It's not like anything worse than my hit and miss in the costume department can happen tonight.....

CHAPTER Two

MIA

THREE YEARS LATER

Resting my head up against the window partially frosted over by the artic temperatures outside, my hot breaths cause a stripe of condensation to form. Pulling back, I use my fingertip to draw a lopsided heart in it, immediately rubbing it away when my own broken heart constricts in my chest. Candice turns up the radio a notch as *John Lennon and Yoko Ono* sing *Happy Christmas* as she comments with a random *Beatles* fact. Candice is a fun fact hoarder and specially equipped for any and all pub quiz nights. I suck on the freshly unwrapped candy cane from the stash in my jacket pocket a little more rigorously, needing the hit of sweetness.

'A little late for all that sugar, no?' Candice sing-songs with pinched brows, I know she's worried about me, hence the impromptu invitation to gatecrash her family Christmas.

'I have no boyfriend, no life and drinking whilst squashed up in the back seat with two children is frowned upon, leave me in peace.'

I bite back defensively. 'It's not like I'm smoking drugs back here, think yourselves lucky that even whilst heartbroken I still retain some bare minimum formalities.' I grin but there is zero warmth in it.

'Sugar is a vice,' Randy adds unhelpfully.

'And a whore is just a prostitute that wasn't smart enough to get paid,' I retort airily, feeling like the *whore* I'm referring to at this moment in time, as I look back on a relationship with nothing to show for the last three years. Neither my best friend nor her now weary husband chooses to argue back, wise decision in my opinion.

Christmas is usually my favourite time of year and as we make our way up the winding slopes of the back streets of the east coast, to Candice's family holiday cabin, the usual miles of leafy green trees are now blanketed a stark white, fitting for this festive time of year. I don't remember asking Santa for heartbreak and gutting sadness this year, but boy did he deliver me a surprise. Walking in on Trevor fucking a literal teenager put new meaning to the stuffing the chicken chore I had tasked him with. He had one fucking job and instead of helping me prepare for our friends coming over early to celebrate Christmas, our last catchup before the new year, when everyone headed out to different ends of the world to visit family for the holidays, he was counting down the hours of my overtime shift. The one I switched out with a co-worker to surprise him. Unwrapping seventeen-year-old Lily and showing his familiarity with the alphabet as he ate her out like a starved man wasn't the sight I had expected when I walked through the front door. I was lucky if he got to E before he got bored between my legs, demanding I blow him because he's had a hard day at work or because my climax last time was clearly stronger than his own. Trevor was many things; a giver wasn't one of them.

'So, are you glad to be getting away?' Candice whispers from the front seat, effectively changing the subject and stroking Randy's hair at the nape of his neck lovingly, sharing a contended glance between their twin two-year-old boys sleeping in their car seats to the side of me. We're all glad they weren't awake for Auntie Mimi's little outburst.

'Let's just say this isn't how I thought my Christmas would be going.' I reply, softening around the edges as my rage level calms to temperamental shrew status.

'Fucking Trevor,' Randy snaps, still quiet enough not to wake the boys, as he navigates the slippery roads, indicating to change lanes as our turn approaches, even though there isn't another car on the road in either direction for miles. 'I know everyone waits until the breakup to say it, but I never liked that guy, you can do so much better Mia,' he adds softly, his apologetic honey brown gaze meeting mine in the rear-view mirror. Randy is a great guy, Candice had met him a week before the carnage of Logan's birthday party, the boys came as a surprise a short time later, but parenthood suits my best friend, the ethereal glow that warms her skin whenever she's around her kids is a joy to witness. I on the other hand have no glow, no little humans and now not even a prick of a boyfriend to call my own. *Merry Fucking Christmas Mia.* The small smile on my face, the show of *thanks for the support* that I can't quite get out verbally, has them titling their heads with pity, a synchronised move I've become all too familiar with since we started our five-hour journey from London. I take it with open arms because right now even that otherwise depressing offering of a sentiment is as close to comfort as I've seen the past six months with Trevor.

'So, what's the plan?' I ask, tamping down the sadness that blooms in my chest like an overinflated balloon ready to pop at any moment.

'Hot chocolate, Christmas movies, some *games*….' Candice begins, lingering on the word games as though it's my turn to fill in the blanks.

'And…' I add, encouraging her to continue with a roll of my hand.

'Wine stupid, buckets of warm, cinnamon scented wine that will keep you permanently on the cusp of festive cheer.' She chortles as though the answer was obvious.

'I like the sound of that,' I coo, watching the snow fall increase as Candice rummages around in her bag for her phone.

'You guys sure you're okay with me encroaching in on your family break?'

'You are family Mills, it's Christmas eve in two sleeps and there was no way I was going to let you stay home and be sad and alone like some spinster.'

'Wow, way to paint a scene babe,' Randy interrupts, vocalising my thought as I imagine such a picture in my head. Although my version has me unwashed, surrounded by cats, with a bottle of vodka in hand, left baron and alone to question all the dumb decisions I had made in my life to get me to that point.

'Thanks Randy, for the show of support,' I say.

'But did I lie?' He responds with a grin.

'No, you did not,' I confer with a snort of a giggle, able to accept defeat when it's banging at my door.

'Look Christmas day we are going to travel to mum and dads for dinner, they wouldn't hear of you not joining us, so let's just enjoy the break. It won't be the Christmas you were expecting but I promise it will be fun.'

It takes me a moment to realise what she's just said, Christmas dinner with her parents.

'Will Logan be there?' I splutter out in a panic. Blink and I would have missed it, but I see Randy and Candice share a knowing glance, their exchange clearly not for me because I don't have a clue what that look is subliminally saying. It's like they are sharing a thought. Clearing her throat Candice turns in her seat to face me, resting her elbow on the centre console.

'The army is keeping Logan overseas for the holidays – at most you will have to enjoy a group video call,' She beams.

'Enjoy?' I chuckle, 'I think you mean endure,' I snort derisively.

'Oh no I think I got it right the first time,' she grins wickedly.

'I DO NOT like Logan,' I protest with a huff, tired of this little idea Candice has been stuck on all these years.

'I'll believe that when your face stops flaming red every time his name is mentioned. I know you thought he was in the wrong at his birthday party that night and that's why you think you hate him, but his opinions on what sort of guy Trevor was, were pretty spot on, recent revelations proof of such.'

I don't tell her she's right even though she clearly is. Logan is never really far from my mind, even though I haven't seen him in what feels like forever. It's the 21st century and I'll admit I have on occasion dabbled in the odd bout of online stalking where Logan Sinclair is concerned. If I had a wank bank, it would be inundated with the pictures that gorgeous human posts. Being stationed overseas for the majority of the past three years, most of the photos are of him on Humvees donning a green camouflage print uniform with desert sand dune backdrops, laughing with fellow comrades. Thankfully what I don't see much of is the usual crowd of women hanging off his arms that I was used to back in the day.

'How Logan handled everything that night, punching Trevor for no good reason, I can't see past that,' I know it's a lie the second it leaves my mouth because I may not have been able to see past his actions at the time, but Trevor showing his true colours puts an entirely different spin on what happened.

'Logan is a brute, handsome, stunning and gorgeous maybe, but still a brute,' I continue, my statement lacking in the believable category. The glint of a sarcastic *okay* in my friends' wide eyes says it all as she turns in her seat to resume her position. Clearly not sold on my utterly hilarious work of fiction. The truth of it is, Logan has always seen me as Candice's annoying little friend, the one too uncool to know what to wear to a fancy-dress party, the friend that humiliated him in front of everyone by slapping him around the face and storming off. No, it's readily clear that I am too chicken shit to admit that I'm scared that he despises the ground I walk on, and why shouldn't he.

The holiday home I had visited every summer from the age of eight to eighteen comes into view as Randy manoeuvres the car up the steep hill leading up to two wrought iron gates that protect the property.

Thoughts of Logan and what transpired the night of his birthday dissipate as the gates swing open and Randy drives up to the house via the cobbled driveway. I'll save thoughts of a particular brooding hot-as-fuck soldier, who I will not mention again for this entire trip, for when I'm alone later, curled up in bed with my hand between my legs.

SHUT-IT-DOWN – that little inner voice warns, and I'm inclined to agree with her because aroused is not a suitable expression right now. I trudge up the marble front steps, careful not to slip as I take each one like a newborn doe. The two black Labradors, Bob and Ross, that Randy had set free from the back of the hatchback bundle past me. Candice and Randy follow suit, trusting the grip of their wellies on the snow-covered steps, each holding a toddler tight to their chests. With flushed pudgy cheeks pressed onto their parents' shoulders the boys continue to wander through dreamland, utterly unaware of their change in surroundings, the bright white lights of the bustling cityscape they are used to no longer in view.

I follow Candice and Randy over the threshold, dumping my bag in the grandeur foyer decorated to the nines like a scene right out of some eighties Christmas movie, wreaths around every frame on the walls and winding trellises of ivy decorated with pinecones and miniature candy canes on the banister of the stairs and over the doorways.

'The twins get our old room Mills, so you're left with your nemesis-slash-lovers room,' she teases, poking me in the ribs and making me jolt.

'Not my nemesis. I bite back, 'or my lover' I tag on quickly when her eyebrows raise in surprise at my retort. Christ how does thoughts of Logan have me so turned around; my brain is a frazzled mess. It doesn't help that I'm going to be sleeping in his bed, in a room filled with his things, the one room I was never allowed to venture into when we were kids. Randy and Candice share the same knowing look they had in the car earlier and I school my expression, too afraid I might be giving something away without realising it.

It's four nights, you only have to sleep in Logan's bed for four nights, you can do this Mia, get a fucking grip. I remind myself, stoking the dimly lit fires of courage that are flickering inside me, even though I know this is more than likely the worst idea imaginable.

CHAPTER
Three

MIA

Tucked up in Logan's sheets, his plump pillow still magically holding the barest scent of him, I allow myself a moment to let my brain wander to thoughts of what my life might have looked like if I had listened to Logan's explanation that night. I had never intended to make Logan Sinclair my enemy, and now that I've seen Trevor for what he is, for what he has probably always been, I'm realising I've wasted the last three years being angry with Logan for no good reason. The stab of guilt settles uneasily in the pit of my stomach as I shuffle over onto my other side, bright wisps of light from the full moon cast streaks across my face and chest as I peer out at the almost black sky. The open tartan curtains billow as the flash of the artic winds flows through the partially open top window, it's refreshing as it tickles my flushed skin and I'm grateful for the sensation when my thoughts once again travel to him. Kicking back the covers and rubbing my bare arms I approach the window and glance out into the back garden, every inch covered with a thick dusting of brilliant white snow. A memory I hadn't thought about for so long hits me, and I suck in a shuddering breath, as I peer into the now weathered ramshackle wooden treehouse outside Logan's bedroom window. The last time I was here during the winter, it was the Christmas break I had almost allowed myself to admit the truth about my feelings for Logan, I had sat in that treehouse, with the boy with the captivating emerald green eyes that I so often got lost in. The prominent scar slashed through his brow didn't belong on the face of this younger version of Logan though, because this was the day he would officially receive that scar, it is the only physical reminder of that day.

FIVE YEARS EARLIER

Eartha Kitt's 'Santa Baby' filters out of the open kitchen window below, where our mothers are gossiping and pulling the last of the gingerbread cookies out of the oven, I was thankful for the melodic tune as it sufficiently masked the thumping of my overworked heart. At seventeen I was the only girl I knew that hadn't already kissed a boy, naive as I was, I hadn't done much of anything really with the opposite sex, and after three weeks of watching Logan swim in the heated indoor pool and walk around the cabin topless wearing just those grey sweatpants and a smile, I lost all semblance of critical thinking and did the unthinkable. Sitting on the floor across from him as he thumbed through a magazine, the material of my denim dungarees scuffed from the climb up the slatted boards pinned to the tree trunk, I cleared my throat dramatically to get his attention. I swallowed the breath thick with trepidation that lodged uncomfortably in my throat. The Michelin man winter coat my mother forced me to wear was a less than preferred outfit choice for what I was about to propose.

Shifting further into the small space I watched as he turned up the little heater beside him. I slid out of my coat and changed position, edging a little closer to Logan as I took a seat on the fluffy flower print beanbag next to him. I pulled nervously at the frayed knees of my dungarees and tried to categorise my panicked thoughts. I had no idea what to even say to him. My anxious behaviour got his attention and he threw aside the magazine, with an arched brow, sans the scar for now, he eyed me curiously, trying to read me, the makings of a question lingering on his full lips as he moved to sit up, pushing the sleeves of his white & tan baseball shirt up his forearms, that notably had far less artwork and far less defined muscles than they do now. Present Logan had blossomed.

'Kiss me' I blurted, adding a tense 'please' that was almost silent. My lungs burned, as my heart clawed at my ribcage, desperate for freedom to dodge the inevitable heartbreak heading its way when Logan would dismiss me. The fear of his rejection made my skin tingle, my lower lip that was pinched between my teeth almost bruising under the pressure.

'Here I was thinking you hated me,' he replied with a shit eating grin as he watched me with a curious interest.

I completely ignored his comment and continued on, worried that if I didn't I would have scrapped the whole idea entirely and ran from the treehouse with my tail between my legs. 'I haven't done it yet, everyone else has and you are pretty much the only guy that doesn't make me want to throw up in my mouth,' I retorted, my proposition sounding far too formal, my voice a little whinier than I had intended and showing my age.

Pinching his lower lip between his thumb and forefinger he appeared to mull over the idea. I'm two weeks shy of my eighteenth birthday and being four years older than me I know there is a very real chance Logan will just laugh in my face and send me packing. But the regret of not asking him before heading back to school with no tales of romance like the other girls, spurs me on to find that sliver of boldness inside myself.

'What's in it for me?' he asked as he shifted across the cherry wood-stained slats beneath us, close enough that his intoxicating scent assaulted my senses, I silenced the needy whimper that formed in my throat before it could escape my lips, before he could read my longing expression. I mirrored his position and moved onto my knees opposite him, desperate to reach out and touch him, but knowing I wouldn't.

'Look I could use the help, I'll owe you,' I said, just about gathering my wits when he leaned in a little closer, intrigue colouring his eyes with flecks of an intense amber. His lips curled up at the edges, the promise of my owing him a favour in return obviously too juicy to pass up. Leaning in, to the point I was sure he could feel my heartbeat through my shirt, he closed his eyes. Even on our knees he towered over me. Something in me snapped and at the last second before our lips could meet, I dodged out of the way. As though everything happened in slow motion I watched as Logan continued to move forward with his eyes closed. The bubble of nerves had caused me to panic. It wasn't that I was anxious about the actual kiss, but rather what it would mean if I liked it, if I finally let my guard down and admitted that I liked him.

Logan face-planting the crudely fashioned bark table wasn't how I saw my first encounter with a boy going, and that damn scar will never let me forget the time I almost had a piece of Logan Sinclair, a romantic first I know I would have treasured.

<u>PRESENT DAY</u>

My gaze drifts to the photo standing proudly on the bedside table of Logan and Candice celebrating at one of his rugby games, his broad form covered in mud and grass stains. I refrain from running my fingers over the image because I'm no longer that seventeen-year-old girl smitten with her best friend's older brother.

I think… my brain begins, ready to give her opinion on how deluded I am, but I shut her down.

'I think it was an epically poor decision to stay here in this room', I scathingly counter aloud before I grab the pillow with the lingering scent of him ingrained in the fabric and press my face into it, screaming until my chest burns with the exertion, the sound thankfully muffled enough as I don't hear footsteps approaching out in the hallway once I'm done. Fuck my life.

MIA

Waking up in Logan's room, I realise I didn't get the best look at everything last night, after a glass of the mulled wine Candice had packed in the thermos for when we got here, and my little trip down memory lane, I was wiped.

Five hours in a cramped back seat with two sticky kids will do that to you. Not that I'm complaining, my Godsons Beau and Blake are awesome, I ignored the fact that they resembled their uncle Logan with their intense muddy green eyes, dark hair, dimpled cheeks and full lips. Damn that man and his strong familial genes. I took a quick shower when I pulled a couple of sugary cheerios from a curl of my hair and collapsed onto the freshly made sheets, drowning in the faint scent of all things Logan, secretly hating how safe and comforted I felt in his bed after so long of trying to push him from my mind.

Was you pushing him out of your mind in the early hours of this morning when you were touching yourself under the covers, as you mumbled out his name? That little voice in my head adds and I choose

to ignore the truth of exactly what she is referring to as I busy myself with the task of unpacking what I need for the day. Finger fucking myself to thoughts of my hot as hell arch nemesis wasn't how I had planned to start off this festive getaway.

I slide the zip open on my case, gearing up to get settled and put my things away. The heavy mirrored wardrobe door whines on its stable like hinges as I slide it open. I find some of Logan's clothes hanging in there and decide it's probably best to live out of my suitcase for the duration of our trip, I'm already invading his space, makes no difference that he's not here to witness it, unpacking and getting comfy in here feels like a step too far. I unpack the essentials, namely my oversized travel washbag and set it down on the counter in the black tiled en-suite, hanging my towel on the brass fixtures beside the walk-in shower. The rumblings of pent-up energy still continue to flare to life in my extremities when I see Logan's aftershave and various other grooming items stacked on the shelves.

Don't you dare. The terse order is a thought I really want to disobey. Whatever this is that I am feeling is not healthy, this level of obsession a little too stalkerish even for me. Mentally berating my reflection in the mirror, I fluff out my wavy red hair and readjust my shorts, the skimpy pyjamas I'm wearing suddenly feeling too tight against my skin. I unzip my washbag, pulling out my little pink plastic friend that has been left inside it since my trip away with Trevor a few months back. *I mean I could.* I immediately question myself, realising that pleasuring myself in Logan's room is far more imposing than hanging my clothes alongside his in the wardrobe. The irony of the bunny ear shaped section of the vibrator and his nickname for me makes me chuckle and I shake my head, throwing the vibrator down on the counter while I search for my travel toothbrush.

———————

I walk back into the bedroom, toothbrush hanging from my mouth, when I stop dead in my tracks. Standing in the middle of the room is Logan, dressed in a relaxed pair of camo trousers, a black short sleeve tee, with a matching camo print cap worn backwards on his head. His clunky black boots are laced up around his ankles, his smart navy Lieutenants uniform perfectly pressed and slung over one shoulder, a green holdall over the other and a wide beaked cap tucked under his arm. I struggle to catch my breath with him looking all kinds of delicious, like a living breathing personification of a ripped GI Joe. It takes me a moment to see the thong suspended from the end of his finger. A giddy smile stretches across his stupidly handsome face as our eyes meet, and I realise the thong in question is one of mine. *Of course it is.*

'What are you.....' I manage to get out, wrapping the silky kimono around my body to hide the fact that I slept in booty hugging shorts and a crop top, my midriff still on show through the sheer material. A sigh of relief tumbles from my mouth when I remember that the only reason I didn't sleep naked like I usually would, is because I was in his bed, this little impromptu reunion could have been more awkward it seems. Thank the Lord for small mercies. Realising I have a little luck on my side does nothing to dampen the misplaced rage building inside me.

'Get the fuck out, Soldier boy!' I bark, all the colour draining from my face as he continues to dangle the lacy material in front of me teasingly. *I shouldn't be this turned on right now.* I lunge at him and grab for my underwear to no avail. He pulls his hand back at the last second and I petulantly stamp my foot in frustration.

'Well hello to you too Bunny. Here I was thinking this was my bedroom.' He states coolly, emphasis on his referral of me when he chances a glance at my lips, the lower one trapped nervously between my teeth as I bite down hard enough to almost break the skin.

'Shit.' Is the only word my brain can come up with in response. I rush to pick up my clothes from yesterday that are strewn haphazardly across the floor, neatening the bed covers. Throwing my belongings into my suitcase I struggle to engage the zip, when I finally get it closed, I straighten my spine and walk towards him. His wicked smile remains as he stands stoically, glancing down my body where the robe has fallen open in my rush to escape. My body aches to be closer to his, but I shake away the urge.

'Logan.' I nod my head, finally acknowledging his presence in a more genial manner as I stroll past him and high tail it around the partition wall to the door. The fort knocks locks screwed into the thick wood are reminiscent of a hotel room as I slide them to the side and open the door, tugging my suitcase behind me. The door shuts behind me with a thud, almost snapping at my heels, I lean back against it and fight the urge to breakdown here in the hallway. A flush of interest at merely being in his presence has a suffocating warmth blooming in my chest.

'*Well hello to you too Bunny*' I say quietly in a whiny voice, mocking Logan and his chirpy greeting. 'Fuck, Bunny' I balk, dread filling my body as I spin on my bare feet and hammer my knuckles against the door in a panic, any thoughts of my thong are long gone as fear constricts my windpipe, when I realise what I forgot to pick up in my haste to get out of the room. The last thing I need is Logan discovering my vibrator in his bathroom. I will never live down the bunny name once he catches sight of the pink plastic bunny shaped accessory that I've relied on for the past three years, my only source of pleasure where orgasms were concerned. I press my ear up against the wood, but I can't hear a thing.

Maybe he didn't see it? Maybe I can get in there before he does. Beating against the door relentlessly my hand begins to throb. Magic in the form of a bright idea smacks me in the face and I haul up my handbag, rummaging around the pointless array of bits and bobs inside until I find the key Candice had given me last night. 'Yes', I holler as I shove it into the lock, my suitcase trailing behind me as I get it open and rush inside. The powerful drum opening of '*The Summoning*' by *Sleep Token* fills the air from the bathroom speakers as the spray of the shower beats against the glass divide.

I leave my case by the entrance and scoot towards the bed, sneaking across the carpet on tiptoes as I approach the bathroom, the door is partially open as balmy steam wafts out from the shower, the mirror misted up as I peer in, the woodsy scent of his body wash, that I recognise as the scent from his pillow tickles my nose.

Looking around I see what I'm after propped up behind my wash bag. Reaching in I keep an eye on the mirror and that's when I see him, every gloriously naked inch of Logan's distorted reflection. Rippling muscles on his heavily tattooed torso flex, his strong hand gripped onto the top of the glass partition, the other moving languidly from the base of his impressive cock to the tip, what looks like black lace secured around his fist, the water cascading down his body disguising the sound of his movements. I snap my mouth closed as I almost sigh at the sight I have dreamt about for so many years. My imagination did not do this man the justice he deserved. My bare feet are glued to the spot, my jaw slack. I should leave, I should run as fast I can from this man, out of this room and as far away from this house as my legs will carry me. Do I do any of that? No, I don't. But why you might ask? Well, it's what he says next that has me losing control of my ability to move a muscle. One word that tethers me to this moment, imprinting a memory I hope I will never forget in my mind.

'Mia,' He growls. My name sounds foreign falling from his full parted lips. Even before he graced me with my fluffy nickname, he had always referred to me as Mills, like everyone else did. This feels like a cry of ownership somehow. Picking up his pace he rests his forehead against the glass, his statuesque profile rigid, hot breaths hitting the glass and his eyes closed tight, as he chases his release over that cliffs edge. 'Fuck, fuck, fuuuuccccckkkk' He roars, and I shudder at the guttural sound of it, every nerve in my body lit up like a fourth of July fireworks display, a detonation of my own twisting up low in my belly. It isn't nearly as rampant of a release as his was, but satisfying enough, as my arousal dampens my sleep shorts, my nipples in stiff peaks as they push against my top. Everything feels too sensitive, my balmy skin covered in goosebumps as my fingers itch to push open the door and join him.

Gathering my senses, I back up into the bedroom on shaking legs, all thoughts of what I actually came in here to retrieve a distant memory after what I've just witnessed. *He said my name, MY name.* As I reach the door and grab for the handle a knock rings out, backing away like a cautious cat I struggle to come up with a plan for my next move. The fight or flight impulse has me near ready to combust as I hear the shower shut off. I fall to the floor and scramble to hide under the bed. I considered the wardrobe but figured he would need clothes after his shower. Even in panic mode the self-preservation kicked in.

All I have to do is wait until he leaves. Possibly easier said than done. I note as an afterthought when I find an old sock tucked away between the leg of the bed and the side table.

I can see in the reflection of the floor to ceiling mirrored wardrobe as Logan jogs across the room, a fluffy navy towel secured around his waist, droplets of water running in rivulets down and over his washboard abs. His dog tags clink together as he hurries to greet whoever it is on the other side of the door making such a racket. His meaty hand runs through his short dark hair shorn close to his scalp on the side and longer on top, causing the muscles down the side of his torso to contract. I slap a hand across my mouth as the makings of a hoarse whimper threatens to fall from my lips. Stuck under a bed and

35

swooning after Logan with cum between my thighs wasn't where I saw my day going when I woke up this morning.

'Where is she? Candice caterwauls, rearranging the pillows on the bed like I will miraculously appear in her fruitless search of the room.

'I've got her cuffed to the radiator in the bathroom, just waiting to have my merry way with her,' Logan snaps back, even though his tone is laced with sarcastic intent, my core thrums at the idea. That statement shouldn't turn me on, but it does. Trevor was always so vanilla in his sexual preferences, outside of some spicy books and the odd skin flick, alone time with my plastic bunny friend was the only time I got off. My sex-life with Trevor had been about as adventurous as suggesting alphabetti spaghetti as a gourmet meal. I bet Logans' a rocky road dessert with sprinkles, smothered in a luxurious gooey chocolate sauce topped with one of those sparkler candle displays kind of lover. I push away the food analogies, sensing the action not only between my legs but in my soon to be grumbling belly. If they find me here, the game is up.

'I can't believe you kicked Mills out,' Candice shrilly retorts, moving across the room to give the bathroom a quick once over just in case he's got me stowed away behind the heated towel rack.

'I didn't kick her out, she ran out because I turned up, very different things Miss know-it-all. Look, she can have my room, I just wanted a shower and there's two little gremlins in the main bathroom. I've been stuck on a plane for hours, didn't get in until five this morning and sleeping on the sofa with Bob and Ross whilst warm, was unpleasant to say the least. And anyways, I didn't even know she was going to be here until I found her sleeping in *MY* bed,' he protests, and I suddenly feel a little guilty for being so standoffish towards him.

'I didn't know you were coming home, mum didn't say anything.' She croons stepping further into the room and fiddling with her car keys in her hand.

'It was meant to be a surprise,' Logan chuckles as he walks over towards his chest of drawers to retrieve a pair of boxers.

Fuck – I internalise the word and the desire to groan at my own stupidity, when Logan's finger runs over the stack of lacy underwear atop his dresser, yet more of my things that I had forgot to pack in my haste to leave. Any normal person would forget a toothbrush, or maybe a pair of socks, oh not me, I forget a nine-inch vibrator and my festive coloured lingerie. His cheeks dimple as the flash of a smile crosses his face before he closes the drawer and makes his way around the bed. I watch as he slides the wardrobe door open, instinctively closing my eyes when his feet are close enough that I could reach out and touch them if I wanted to, my five-year-old way of thinking that if I can't see him then he can't see me my only line of defense right now. Logan turns to face Candice.

'Are you going to leave and let me get dressed?' He grumbles as she fiddles with the dark locks of her side plait.

'No, what are your intentions with Mills?' Candice demands as she crosses her arms across her chest and I'm suddenly calm, interested to know what his answer will be.

'I've got no idea what you are talking about,' His voice is notably an octave higher and I'm glad to see in the reflection of the mirror that Candice noticed it too, as a grin forms on her pink painted lips.

'Oh, so we're all still denying this thing between the two of you. Delusional much? I tell you what, I've decided I'm giving you both a freaking clue as a gift this Christmas. It's cheap, cheerful and it's the gift that keeps giving. You like her.' She accuses. A statement rather than a question.

'She's like my stepsister,' He argues, and I bite back the bile rising in my throat, my distaste for the otherwise sweet sentiment making me want to crawl out from under this bed and slap some sense into him.

Shower antics aside he isn't entirely wrong. We hate each other, right? I mean we grew up together. To the outside world he is as close to a brother as I'm ever going to get.

My brain kicks in with an unhelpful retort – *So we're all lying out of our arses today then?*

'She's like your stepsister as much as Trevor was her soulmate.' Candice chuckles and I see Logan's fists clench at the mere mention of my ex. I don't hate his reaction and neither does my belly as it does a little giddy flip at the air of possessiveness that radiates from his tense broad shoulders.

'Must be hard to know he has had her for the past three years.' She adds just to rile him up. He doesn't answer his sister, but it's hard to miss the sharp growl of disgust that falls from his lips, even from my position tucked under the bed.

Logan turns and grabs a rolled up black t-shirt out of his holdall, shrugging it on whilst his other hand fists the towel wrapped around his waist.

'She isn't here, I don't know what to tell you.' He retorts haughtily as Candice scans the room again. Shuffling towards the dresser he sneakily slides open the top drawer and sweeps my underwear into it when her back is turned.

'Don't even bother Logan, I have two sons and I can scan a room in 1.3 seconds upon entry. I saw the underwear that clearly isn't yours the second you opened the door; I've got eyes in the back of my head – one of the perks of motherhood.' She chuckles, hitting him with a raised brow, her schooled features oozing superiority.

'That and the need to know everything that isn't your business it seems. You turn into mum more with each visit little sis.' Logan snickers, because he knows Candice's biggest fear is turning into their mother.

'The fact that there is a wet thong on the side in the bathroom raises some questions,' she continues with wide eyes & a slick smile. She refuses to bite back at him the way he had wanted, he could try and distract her as much as he wants, my best friend is like a dog with a bone when it comes to the conversation of him and I. I should know after her monthly interrogations. My gaze settles a little too long on Logan's face as he continues to profess every reason why Candice is wrong in her assumptions of how he might feel about me, so long in fact that I don't realise Candice is staring directly at my reflection in the wardrobe mirror, a giddy expression plastered on her beautifully made-up face. Before she can turn to Logan and out me, I press my index finger to my lips, silently begging her to keep her mouth shut. She does without question, her promise to always have my back clearly outweighs her desire to mess with her brother.

'What's the smile for?' Logan asks her, suspicion heavy in his voice.

'Oh nothing,' She beams wickedly, the Cheshire wide grin unmovable on her face as she likely mentally plans our June nuptials. She has been waiting years for us two to finally trudge up the courage to admit how we feel, ever since she caught me that summer when we were fourteen, when I was mooning over him from the treehouse as he practised his rugby trick shots below on the green.

'I know that look Candice, whatever wayward idea you are mulling over, forget it.' Logan chimes in as he reaches for his leather bike jacket that is slung over the tartan armchair. Even with his imposing Lieutenant tone, that he usually reserves for the troop of soldiers under his command, everyone currently in this bedroom knows she won't.

'Hurry up and get dressed, the boys want to show you something.' She cajoles, chomping at the bit to pull me out from under the bed to find out everything she can. There is only one thing that can make my best friends eyes shine as brightly as they are right now.....gossip.

'Are you going to leave and let me get ready?' He asks for the second time since his sister entered his space.

'Nope. Go get changed in the bathroom, you'll move a little quicker knowing I'm waiting.'

I watch as Logan retreats into the bathroom, that scowl of annoyance meant solely for his sister souring his expression. We likely have a maximum of three minutes until he ushers her out of this room and locks the door behind them, five minutes if he hasn't brushed his teeth. All the years of Candice pranking Logan has made him suspicious, hence the fort knocks dead bolt entrance security. He had good reason to distrust her after waking up with a sharpie cock and balls scribbled on his cheek on picture day, he swore she would never get him again and that's when their dad agreed to the locks. A buzzing sound from the bathroom seconds my earlier thought of Logan brushing his teeth. Candice can use the fact that he will purposefully prolong her waiting in the hopes of annoying her, giving her time to interrogate me as to why I am hiding out under her big brother's bed seemingly without his knowledge.

'Details,' she whispers eagerly with a roll of her wrist as I scramble out from under the bed, almost snagging a wayward curl of my red hair on the frame as I do. When I don't answer her immediately, much to her annoyance, she takes up a motherly stance, crossing her arms over her chest again with an expectant gaze. It does the job because I'm quick to fill in the blanks.

'Nothing is going on.' I protest, whisper yelling as I throw panicked glances towards the closed bathroom door. She doesn't believe me for a second. 'I left some stuff in here and used the key to get in. When I heard Logan coming out of the bathroom I panicked and hid.' I'm flustered, a flappable mess, but she's still eyeing me shrewdly, her wide eyes still flitting to the closed door that separates us from Logan and then back to me, I see the moment she realises my explanation is for the best part true when her hardened gaze softens, her pursed lips

41

relaxing. I can see the cogs working in her brain, she knows there is something I'm clearly holding back, she knows me too well not to see the truth, but for now I know considering the time constraints, she will leave it be and make a mental note to discover what it is later.

Oh, I caught your brother jacking off in the shower whilst using my thong as a sex aid and calling out my name. Yeah, I think I'll be keeping that little nugget of truth behind clenched lips for as long as I can.

'I made breakfast,' Candice calls out to Logan as she steps aside and gestures for me to make my escape. I just about make it out of the door when I hear Logan stepping out of the bathroom.

CHAPTER
Five

LOGAN

I stroll into the dining room with Beau wrapped around one leg and Blake saddled on my back, his stubby little arms holding on for dear life around my neck and briefly cutting off my airway as he tightens his grip when he scrambles to wrap his little legs around my torso.

'Good morning, Randy. Always nice to see you mate.' I say approaching my brother-in-law and pulling him into a bear hug. Blake uses this opportunity to lunge at his father and his dad is prepared and luckily catches him mid-leap. Beau, bored that his ride is over, and I'm now standing still, follows suit and repositions himself around his father's leg.

'Glad to finally have you home. It was a surprise, to all of us,' Randy states, struggling against the instinct to look Mia's way. The thought of coming home for Christmas and keeping it a secret from everyone but my mother was fun, as I hadn't been home in well over eight months, but adding Mia to the mix made it downright exhilarating. I won't lie, I had spent so many nights away thinking about the girl with the waves of deep auburn hair, mesmerising seawater-blue eyes and hourglass figure. The fact that she is currently scowling at me from across the dining room table, where she stands with a hot mug of coffee, her leg propped up against the kitchen counter that breaks up the open plan space, does nothing to soften my interested gaze. The intense heat radiating off of her is either nervousness or hatred, or maybe a mix of the two, I haven't seen her for three years so it's hard to tell. But I can't for the life of me think why she would be nervous in my company, so I settle on the latter assumption, pure unadulterated hate.

Why is it that I find bratty Mia so beguiling.

'Bunny, you look lovely,' I state, masking my compliment with a sarcastic edge just to fuck with her as I pull out a chair and take a seat at the table beside Randy. I have a sneaking suspicion she doesn't hate the nickname I gave her all those years ago as much as she says she does. I watch as her cheeks redden under the smattering of cute freckles on her face.

This weekend is going to be fun.

My hooded gaze travels the length of her, admiring the curve of her arse in those tight fit denim jeans as she reaches for a candy cane to stir her drink, the fullness of her breasts contained in the oversized knitted jumper that hangs off one shoulder, adds a preppy feel to her whole ensemble as it's finished off with a pair of impeccably clean white Converse. It's a look I wouldn't usually consider my type, but there is just something about her, an energy that goes beyond what she chooses to wear. I run my thumb across the slit in my eyebrow, the

44

injury she caused the last time she tried to run away from me up in the treehouse. The squeak of understanding that *My Bunny* unintentionally lets out has my cock twitching in my pants. I'm grateful for the distraction of Randy trying to impress me with the statistics from his fantasy league football tournament. I don't miss my use of the reference *My Bunny.* Mia has never and will never be my girlfriend, she's made that perfectly clear, it didn't help that I tried to rearrange her now ex-boyfriend's face three years ago, this girl can hold a grudge.

'Still have that sweet tooth I see,' I chuckle as I watch Mia suck on the end of the candy cane secured between her full lips, silently wishing she'd let me give her something else to suck so enthusiastically on.

'Tis the season,' she snaps back and fuck if the gravelly edge of her retort doesn't make me want to outwardly groan. I'm thankful the tabletop is hiding the fact that my cock is tenting in my pants like I'm a teenager again, unable to control himself. My thoughts flit back to her standing half naked in my room this morning and I shift in my seat.

'Would you like some?' She teases as she leans across the table, holding out the candy to me with a slick grin before Randy rightly reads the building tension between us and calls out *'be right there'*, pretending Candice had summoned him just so he can escape. His uneasiness seems to pull Mia from her uncharacteristic flirty behaviour, and I hate the shock of reality that filters into her mossy rimmed sea-water blue gaze. The 180-degree flip in her mood completely obliterates the live wire of lust that just moments ago had seemed to tether us. I fight the urge to climb over the table and pull her up into my arms, to tell her that whatever this is between us is okay, because while I want nothing more than to bathe in her warmth and forget everything else around me, nothing good can come from exploring this. I watch her busy herself in the kitchen as she pours herself another cup of coffee, purposefully dodging my gaze. If I had done things differently three years ago, if I had told her the truth, maybe....

'Logan. Delivery,' Candice caterwauls from the hallway, interrupting my train of thought and I'm up and out of my seat, thankfully sans the growing erection.

The greying man slumped over the pile of brown boxes is wheezing, the tips of his fingers blue and a dusting of frost clinging to his long shaggy beard. Randy rushes past me with a steaming mug of coffee for the man who looks like he's on the brink of collapse.

'Stu, where is your truck?' I ask, grabbing my scarf and hat off the coat hook, squatting down on my haunches, and proceeding to dress the man for the brutal elements.

'Had to park down the lane on the main road,' he says breathily between sips of his coffee. 'The roads are snowed over, wouldn't be safe to try driving up here.' The pang of guilt that hits me is clearly visible in my expression. 'No apologies necessary kid, I couldn't let you go without Christmas presents.' Stu chuckles, patting me on my shoulder. Having been our postman since I was ten, he has always referred to me as Kid, even now when I tower over him, easily twice his size in both height and width.

'Let's hope it was worth it, I'm not known for my gift selection skills.' I retort, smiling broadly when I remember the last-minute gift I had ordered for Mia, after my mother had told me she would be visiting for Christmas. I had lied to my sister, I knew all along that Mia would be here at the cabin, it was my main reason for asking my superior for the early extended leave.

Cloaking him in every possible extra layer that we could, including my hat, scarf, and gloves that I refused were mine when he tried to give them back, we waved Stu off down the pathway through the tall trees. Every surface of the usually autumnal colour scheme of the wilderness surrounding the cabin is now a stark white, the level of the ground rising as the snow continues to fall. Looks like we're here for the long haul.

CHAPTER Six

MIA

Candice helps me repack my suitcase into an orderly fashion in her room, the same room we shared every summer as teens, the twin beds I remember so fondly now swapped out for a king-size four poster bed kitted out with *Henry the eighth* drapery. I've finally cleared all signs of myself out from Logan's space. After seeing Logan in the shower this morning and our little interaction over the dining table, running away feels like the only option. Crazy as it seems in hindsight, I had chosen Trevor's love, or what I thought was love, over Logan's feelings three years ago at his birthday party, mainly because nineteen-year-old me could never imagine he would reciprocate my feelings. I settled for Trevor's arse grabbing and crude comments because I thought that was all I deserved. I remember that desolate notch of disbelief that swamped Logan's expression when I laid into him after he beat Trevor so viciously. Even though at first glance Logan looks imposing with his broad shoulders, inked skin, and his looming height, I had only ever seen the softness in him. The caring, thoughtful boy who was happy to save his little sister's friend from social suicide by being her first kiss, the guy surrounded by beautiful women that made a point in telling me, that I too looked just as beautiful. But that night, the feral beast Logan held back was set free and Trevor took a beating. Apparently, all because Trevor dared to comment on Logan's playboy actions. I swore in that moment that any feelings I may have harboured for Logan would never again resurface. It was a mistake to come here. In the light of discovering the shitty man Trevor is I'm questioning everything from that night. Was I too naive, too dumb to investigate what had happened between Logan and Trevor? Would I have listened to Logan if he had tried to reach out to me after it happened?

'I think it's best if I leave,' I mumble. Keeping all the other worries rumbling around in my brain to myself.

'Tough luck cookie, old man Stu says we're snowed in for the foreseeable future. We will be able to walk over to my mum's house the day after tomorrow if we go through the forest, but the roads are a no-go. Sorry.'

There isn't even a hint of genuine apology in her voice as she continues to fold one of my hoodies, a playful grin tugging at the corners of her lips.

A cover of *'Baby it's cold outside'* that I don't recognise plays from downstairs, the irony of the lyrics not lost on me.

'Do we need music on 24/7?' I snap grumpily, ready to put a cease and desist on any and all Christmas cheer, while I catalogue all the reasons why staying here in this house with Logan is a really shitty idea.

'It's a time to be jolly, don't start ragging on the soundtrack to this most wonderful holiday season and pouting because the universe is trying to send you a message, there are worst places you could be right now,' She states.

'Yeah, namely under Trevor,' I offer, finally seeing her point as a shudder of revulsion rockets through my torso. How I had stayed with him as long as I had was borderline insanity.

'We're trapped here, so you might as well deal with it. Preferably in a timely fashion, because this whole awkward, I don't know where to look game between you and Logan, is making me want to lock you both in a cupboard and demand you air out your grievances with a therapeutic game of seven minutes in heaven.'

'Oh God,' I groan, both hating her tone yet loving her idea. I'm just a ball of wired emotions and untapped sexual expression right now.

'Look, it's not that bad, Logan even got you a Christmas present.' She adds, beaming at me with a mischievous smirk, knowing that I won't ask if she knows what he got me, but that I will make it my mission to overthink the kind gesture until I've turned myself inside out.

'With how much you are enjoying this, I'm questioning our friendship,' I chuckle. Throwing a pair of fluffy socks at her head. She catches them mid-air, unravels them and sits on the edge of the bed, sliding them onto her bare feet.

'Yeah, yeah. I may be girl bossing life but even I don't control the weather.' She snaps back playfully.

I have a sneaking suspicion that even if she could control the weather we would still be stuck in this situation. Candice is determined that Logan and I hash out whatever it is that makes the air fizzle with unrest when we are in the same vicinity.

I'm quickly realising, I might want that too.

CHAPTER
Seven

MIA

Sitting on the sofa, my legs tucked up under me, I zone out. Sucking on my fourth candy cane of the day and enjoying the dull thrum of the constant sugar rush flowing through my veins. Stroking Bob's furry body with my free hand, the larger of the two pups, it is oddly relaxing as the tinkering of Christmas music plays in the background. My bah humbug attitude lifting as the hours tick by. The soft warm lights of the decorated fern tree filling the corner of the room and the sound of the crackling fire with the cinnamon soaked wood burning, makes this moment feel like it's been ripped right out of a *Hallmark* movie. When my gaze meets his, as he sits on the floor potato painting festive themed artwork with the twins, I realise it isn't the warmth from the grated fireplace beside me that is causing my body to overheat. I see him glance my way every so often out of my periphery and I only chance a look back at him when I know he is distracted by his nephews. I can't help the smile from spreading across my face when the mountain of a man that exudes Adonis hot vibes, is

finger-painting what I presume from this angle, is Rudolph the reindeer with a bright red bulbous nose, his meaty tattooed hands coated in colourful paint. I add *cute* to my list of descriptors for Logan. The hairs on the back of my neck suddenly stand to attention and I can feel the heat of his gaze directed my way. I lift my chin and we lock our eyes. Hypnotised by the unspoken conversation currently happening between us, a mental image hits me, my brain betraying me once again.

Lieutenant Logan Sinclair in full uniform, the wide brim of his hat dipped low enough to cast a shadow over his hooded green gaze, those tatted hands wrapped around my throat as I kneel at his booted feet. "Want to play Bunny?" He whispers darkly with an air of devilment as his grip tightens over my pulse points, interrupting the flow of blood to my brain and making me lightheaded. Arousal slick between my parted thighs.....

It's impossible to swallow down the audible groan that falls from my lips and as though he knows where my thoughts have taken me, he grins wickedly, his lower lip pulled between his thumb and forefinger, as my cheeks flush a beetroot red. Ross, the ball of fluff with ADHD of the canine variety, jolts in a panic as I jump to my feet. Peering around suspiciously like he's preparing to attack. My shaking legs and heavy core make me unsteady as I sway on my feet. The candy cane I had been sucking on is held between my teeth as I turn on the spot and rush out of the room, speed walking through the kitchen to the other end of the cabin. The cool night air that has penetrated the glass conservatory is exactly what I need to soothe the thrum of heat coating my skin. Logan is far enough away from me that my brain fog begins to lift, and my senses feel more like my own again.

LOGAN

I see the way she is looking at me, there isn't a filter available to hide the flush of needy unrest colouring her skin. I want to spoil her, I want to worship her, I want to completely ruin her in the best kind of way. When my mum told me Mia would be here for the holidays I laughed, quickly denying the truth that my little sister's best friend was all that filled my mind on a regular basis. I told myself I could hack it, that I would be able to get through the next few days, seeing her as what she was, just a family friend – delusion is a funny old thing, thoughts of her naked and writhing under my touch hit me like a plank of wood to the face the second I saw her standing there in next to nothing in my bedroom, her slack jaw and wide honey speckled cerulean eyes filled with surprise only adding fuel to the already out of control forest fire raging inside me. Even with three years apart, once again, this woman has me hypnotised.

I remind myself that she explicitly told me that she didn't want to explore whatever this could have been between us, that deep down she hates me, even though Trevor turned out to be everything and more than I accused him of being. I remind myself that she isn't mine and no amount of dreaming that she maybe could be, will make the reality any different. All that and I still can't help but imagine her in my arms, waking me in the mornings with a needy kiss, jumping into my arms when I come home from deployment. *What the fuck is wrong with me? But what if.* My brain offers when I catch her staring at the exchange I'm having with my nephews. Women go all soft for guys around kids, right? My point is proven when she catches me watching her and she practically rockets out of her seat, a red blush to her cheeks matching her hair that I refuse to believe is from the roaring fire. What has got my little Bunny so wound up?

If I wasn't already contemplating bounding across the room and throwing her over my shoulder, giving her arse cheek a swift slap as I carry her up to my bedroom, then hearing the pleasure laden groan that tumbles from her swollen candy slicked lips is the way to make it happen.

But before I get the chance to throw caution to the wind and playfully taunt her about her reaction as I bundle her up into my arms, she's up and out of the room. My shoulders slump a little as she seemingly takes all of the air from the room with her, a stabbing sensation filling my chest and constricting my ability to take a full breath down into my lungs. I immediately hate that she's no longer within reach. There is a calming aspect to my soul when she is close by, a sensation I've pushed aside and refused to acknowledge before now, a dire attempt to salvage what is left of my overworked brain where all things Mia are concerned.

This girl is going to be the death of me.

CHAPTER
Eight

MIA

I love the excitement that shines from the boys' little cherub faces at the idea of the jolly fat man they expect to shuffle down the chimney and sprinkle the room with gifts. Even though it isn't Christmas Eve until tomorrow, I can hear Logan behind me trying to convince the boys that Santa would actually prefer a glass of single malt whiskey on the festive plate they are preparing to set on the fireplace. It's a practice run they are determined to see through incase Santa decides to show up twenty-four hours early after Randy discussed the realities of Santa's magic and time zone issues over the breakfast table this morning. Beau grabs for the fur trimmed red hat from off the table and pulls it down onto Logan's head, chuckling as his uncle rubs at his short beard and gruffly says 'Ho, Ho, Ho,' with a booming timbre.

The beginnings of a new kink arise, namely Logan wearing a red velvet two piece, the jacket edged with white fluffy trim, open and exposing every one of the ripped muscles I can make out beneath his fitted t-shirts, the matching velvet trousers hanging low enough so that glorious V at his waist is on show. I almost forget how to breathe as a rush of air gets caught in my throat at the thought of Logan ready and willing to give me his *Christmas cheer*, if you know what I mean.

'*The drapes know what you mean for Christ's sake, you're practically dribbling,*' that little inner voice adds, and I swallow down the excess saliva in my mouth and continue to hang the string of cutout paper snowflakes the boys had made above the beamed alcove by the door. Swaying my hips to *Jingle bell rock by Bobby Helms,* I fumble with a tack and it slips from between my fingers, still humming along happily with the popular Christmas song, thoughts of a half-naked Logan set aside, for now, I drop to my knees and rummage around in the shaggy pile rug and between the presents in search. The last thing I'd want is for one of the twins to step on it. As though fate had steered me here, I run a finger across a name tag attached to a hefty box wrapped in holly themed paper with a gaudy red bow atop it. *Dear Bunny...* that's all it reads and there is no way those two simple words should have my belly flip flopping the way that it is. Someone clearing their throat has me falling onto my arse as though I've just been caught doing something I shouldn't be. It takes me a moment to remember I'm a grown-up, it takes me even less time than that to realise it's Logan who has his legs crossed at the ankles leaning up against the living room door frame watching me, that boyish grin fixed in place as always.

'Snooping Bunny?' He questions, before sucking on the end of a candy cane from my hidden stash in the top kitchen cupboard. I hold back the '*fuck*' that builds in my throat in response to the sight of him twisting his tongue around the sweet treat, because if I don't, I will lose any and all deniability that I still have, when it comes to how I feel about this man.

'I dropped a tac; I'm simply searching for it.' I retort, a little more arrogantly than I had intended. I continue rummaging once again on my knees between the wrapped presents to second my explanation. My arm shoots back as pain jolts through my hand and I watch as a trickle of blood starts to roll down my palm, the tac in question now embedded deep in my pointer finger. I let my head fall back as I scowl at the ceiling, silently chastising the universe for its attempt to reinforce my response to Logan as to why I'm crawling around on all fours. *Well played.*

Appearing by my side, standing over me he grabs for a Christmas tree print napkin from off the coffee table, carefully removing the tac he applies pressure to my finger, his warm hand cupping mine, holding it above my head against his waist and causing goosebumps to skitter up my spine.

'Want to know what I got you?' Logan asks, oozing charm as his amber flecked bottle green eyes sparkle with mirth when he gestures to the wrapped gift topped with the tag that has my nickname scribbled on it.

'Not particularly, I can't imagine it's going to be something I want.' I answer airily, gazing up at him, knowing it's a flat out lie. I reckon I would happily sell a kidney right now to know the contents of that box, of the organs available at least I have two of those.

'Oh, you'll want it.' He chuckles, that slice of sternness he usually saves for his time in the military shining through as he lowers himself so he's balancing on the balls of his feet, his hazy gaze dipped in search of mine as his meaty thighs cage me in. I let go of the heavy breath I'm holding on to and look at him, satisfaction warming his features as he licks at the candy again, torturously slow, teasingly so.

With my brows pinched I move to say something petulant in response to him crowding my personal space. He shakes his head to silently warn me against it as he removes the sweet candy from his mouth. My lips part freeing a breathy whimper, and my body betrays me, as it concedes with little argument to his silent command, a fizzle of warmth vibrating up my spine. It takes a second for my brain to engage as I watch him remove the napkin from my skin and wrap his lips around the tip of my bleeding finger. I shudder as he sucks on it and proceeds to pull it free with a wet pop. The feral claiming of something so hedonistic pulling an animalistic groan from my throat.

Unable to hold back a moment longer, my body quivering, something in me snaps and I lunge at him, my lips crashing against his as our tongues lap between nips, licks and kisses. Straddling him, pushing him down, his back now pressed against the carpet, I tighten my thighs around his hips. His calloused hand is bruising as he grips onto the back of my neck, deepening the kiss as his other hand wraps around my waist, tethering me to him, his fingers pressing into my hip enough he's sure to leave a mark. My lungs scream for respite as I struggle to suck in a steady breath between his ardent worshipping kisses. But I'm too engulfed in the moment, too lost in him, too hungry for whatever this is.

'and we don't put popcorn up our nose because…..' Randy asks Beau as he walks into the room, cradling the toddler in his arms. I jump off Logan in one fluid move like a petrified cat doused in water as I paw at my harassed lips, the skin of my jawline raw and sensitive from the scruff of his short beard. Every part of my body he had made contact with tingles, the heat dissipating the longer this moment drags on as I try to right myself.

'What did uncle Logi do Mimi?' Beau asks me, the two-year old's concern as transparent as his father's amusement.

'Uncle Logi and Auntie Mimi have issues to sort through,' Randy offers, unable to drop the smirk. I can see him mentally cataloguing what he just walked in on so he can share a detailed witness account with Candice, she would have his guts if he failed to be specific and we all know it.

'Auntie Mimi wanted a taste of Uncle Logi's candy cane,' Logan coltishly responds, propping himself up and resting back on his elbows with a smug as fuck smirk spread across his annoyingly handsome face. *What a prick.*

'Sharing is caring,' Beau quips and Logan is unable to stifle the roar of laughter from barreling out of his mouth as he quickly gets to his booted feet.

'Ain't that the truth little man.' He chortles as he holds his hands out to his nephew. Making the jump from his father to his uncle I watch as Logan walks out into the kitchen, tickling my cheeky dark-haired Godson under his chubby chin as he goes, thoughts of how much popcorn he can fit up his tiny nose clearly forgotten.

'Well, well, well,' Randy says with raised brows, his tone light. Amusement tugging at his lips.

'I'll have zero judgement from you, remember your wife tells me everything...' I warn with an authoritative jiggle of my index finger in his direction and the smile falls from his face. Smoothing down my clothes to keep my hands busy is about the limit of my brainpower right now, the fires Logan stoked inside me withering into a pile of ash. My traitorous body is desperate to be swathed in his woodsy scent again, to feel his hands grip around my bare skin, to have his palms moulding to the dips and curves of my body. Shaking away the thought with a heavy exasperated exhale, I turn and exit the room on unsteady legs. I bypass the kitchen and take the stairs two at a time up to the shared bathroom. Gripping the black marble counter as I turn on the tap, the steady stream of cold-water splashes against my arms.

'Get a fucking grip. It's Logan. He hit your boyfriend over some stupid male sports bullshit, never called to apologise and hasn't spoken to you in three years. Logan, a man that probably sleeps with anything that doesn't move fast enough and is just toying with you for some sick pleasure that feeds his tortured little soul. He can't have you. You won't let him have you.' I recite the mantra quietly at my reflection, praying at least some of it will stick. The fact that the fading memory of his touch on my skin still has my core clenching is an indicator that I am lying through my arse about it all, but this is a lot to unpack right now. I neither have the mental capacity, emotional strength, nor necessary libido control to address what just happened between us downstairs.

61

CHAPTER *nine*

MIA

I carry on with the job I started earlier and unravel the tinsel from the box to continue decorating the sitting room, keeping myself busy means I'm not sitting across from Logan and pining over what it would be like to have him pressing me face down into a mattress, as he strips me down and feasts on my body. I physically shake away the daydream and the conversation Candice is having with Logan behind me seeps back into existence, as though my hearing had momentarily shut down when I allowed inappropriate thoughts of Logan to steal away my concentration. I'm amazed I'm getting anything done being on lockdown in this cabin with him.

'Dad says it's coming down, it's a shame really, we loved that treehouse. I was kind of hoping the boys might get to enjoy it.' Candice says softly as she hands Beau a spoonful of green icing to decorate the Christmas tree cookies, most of the previous spoonful currently smeared across his rosy cheeks.

'He can't destroy the tree house, that's a part of our childhood, special moments have happened in there...' I splutter, my mouth running away with me as hurt laces my tone. My gaze flicks to Logan and I can't help the blush rising up my neck. His expression softens and I know the memory of our almost first kiss skitters into his head. 'Do you remember sneaking away there to try our first beer at fourteen, and it's where you realised that Tommy Carter didn't want to feel up your boobs because he was gay at fifteen.' I overshoot my sad attempt to glaze over the real reason why I love the treehouse so much and everyone in the room knows it, even my Godson is staring at me with his spoonful of icing resting on his lip as though he can see right through my bullshit.

'Dad says it isn't safe and he has no desire to fix it up, I tried convincing Randy to take on the job but other than a deep tissue massage he isn't exactly what you'd call handy.'

'No lies were told,' Randy concurs with a small smile as he swallows down a mouthful of his beer. I don't think he's ever even hung a photo frame; DIY tasks generally fall in Candice's lap.

'Dad is turning sixty-seven next month so unless you can convince him to hire someone to fix it,'

'Unlikely' Logan chuckles, knowing his father and his frugal ways. That man hasn't paid anyone for a service he could attempt himself in all the years I've known him. The summer Candice turned sixteen was a perfect example, wrangling horses is not a natural talent Mr. Sinclair possesses, he also should never again bake, drive a tractor, reupholster a sofa or change out the pipes under the patio. I decide I have two days to come up with a foolproof plan to convince Mr. Sinclair to loosen his purse strings and hire someone to fix up the tree house. I'll keep my fingers crossed for a Christmas miracle of the impossible kind.

––––––––––

Finishing my fourth glass of home brewed mulled wine I stretch out my legs, shifting on the oversized armchair as the tingling buzz of the alcohol warms in my veins as I stave off sleep. The emotional game of tennis I've been having with Logan today has been exhausting. He looks my way, I look away, and vice versa, the ache in my neck is becoming a problem. I rub it to loosen the knot forming there and groan when the tension momentarily dissipates. Hooded emerald eyes find me as his full lips part. All I can seem to think about is that kiss, about his lips on mine, about his hands roaming over my body. This whole damn situation is confusing and infuriating. Falling for a guy that despises me wasn't on the festive bingo sheet I had in mind for this holiday getaway. I never heard anything from Logan after that night of his birthday party when he attacked Trevor, the excuses of some old Rugby score to settle and Logan's addiction to shagging as many women as possible being two of the many other reasons Trevor gave me for why they fought. But I had never heard Logan's truth on the matter. It was all so childish. I doubt without the added incentive of liquid courage it would even have happened but when the weeks passed and Logan seemed to steadily cut me out of his life, distancing himself on social media where he would usually send funny GIFS or snarky comments, I realised it had meant more to him then I had first thought. Logan detested Trevor, there was no hiding their mutual hate for one another, I just never thought that it was enough of a reason for him to detest me too. Whatever Logan is doing here is a game to him, I need to quickly get on board and decipher his plan because right now, he's playing poker while I'm still sorting pairs in a hand of go fish.

'We're going to head up,' Candice yawns, leaning into Randy's touch as he massages her shoulders. The grandfather clock in the hallway chimes signaling midnight and for the first time this evening, I suddenly remember I have nowhere to sleep. As though the dogs have read my mind they hop up onto the sofa once Randy has vacated his spot, lengthening their shaggy fur bodies across the cushions, claiming it as theirs.

'You can attempt to snuggle in between them, but I wouldn't recommend it, Bob has a twisted colon and Ross has incurable halitosis.' Randy adds unhelpfully with pursed lips, as I consider the pros and cons of putting together a makeshift cot in the coat closet under the stairs.

'Looks like you're in with me Bunny,' Logan retorts, clearly amused as he toys with me.

'Whatever I did in a past life to deserve this level of torture, I repent, I pledge my soul for eternity to whatever entity can clear the roads and get me out of here.' I clap back with a petulant stamp of my foot, hating that my body betrays me and shivers at the thought of sharing a bed with Logan.

'Slightly drastic Bunny, but okay.' He teases.

I scowl at him, trying with everything in me to disguise the smidgen of hope that lingers in my expression, hope that has no business here in this current situation. Holding out an arm towards the door Logan encourages me to take the lead with a shit eating grin on his smug face.

———

I stack the throw cushions in the centre of the bed like they are an impenetrable wall and scoot beneath the covers on the side closest to the door in case I need to make a speedy exit.

'Are you really that worried Bunny, I mean after you kissed me today, I would have thought you would *jump* at the chance to get me in the sack,' He chortles, 'Or hop,' he adds as an afterthought. I don't need to be able to see his face to know he's smiling at yet another reference to my bunny status. His voice may be muffled by the wall of pillows, but his potent manly scent refuses to be contained as it caresses my skin. He's too close.

'You certainly think a lot of yourself there Solider boy, that kiss was a mistake.' I reply bluntly. A bolstered lie I hope he believes. 'And while we're at it, just so you know, I wouldn't willingly jump, hop or otherwise into bed with you unless it was absolutely necessary.' I protest, yet another lie.

'I could put in some earplugs if you fancy some special time with the pink plastic General.' I die a little inside with that comment, vividly remembering the vibrator I had forgotten to stow away in my hurry to leave his room earlier. He had seen it.

'I'll pass, wouldn't want to give you the wrong idea.' I snap back, glad that he can't see my taut expression as I furiously chew on my bottom lip and a flush of embarrassment creeps across my face.

'The ship has sailed with that one, after the show you put on for me last night.' He chortles and suddenly everything in me sinks. A smattering of nervous sweats forming on my hairline as panic grips my heart in a vice like grip.

'It's amazing the apps you can download these days, it sent a notification directly to me, almost totaled my bike when I chanced a look on my way up here.' I could call him a liar, I could storm out of the room and take my chances with the dogs' downstairs, but all that will do is give him the reaction he wants, and caving to Logan Sinclair, just isn't in my DNA.

'Checking your phone whilst driving, you're a moron.' I snap, deciding to ignore his comment and play dumb.

'If you had heard what I had as the notification opened in my pocket you would have risked it too.' He hasn't mentioned that I said his name or that I used my fingers and not the *plastic pink General* as he called it, so a part of me wants to call bullshit. This is likely yet another form of torture for him to use against me to watch me squirm, and damn if it isn't working. I'm grateful for the respite when he turns over and doesn't utter another word. I wait out the silence in the dark room until I hear soft grumbles of exhaustion fall from his lips as sleep claims him. Thanks to a combination of suppressed anger, misplaced lust & alcohol warming my belly, I finally fall asleep myself, huddled as close to the edge of the bed as I can manage without falling out onto the floor. The thought of Logan watching me pleasure myself shouldn't turn me on as much as it does, sadly I have no say in the matter as dreams of him doing exactly that fill my brain.

How to navigate whatever this is growing between Logan and I, is officially future Mia's problem.

CHAPTER Ten

MIA

I wake to a racket from outside, the clunk and thwack of metal on wood making my head throb. *Coffee, I need coffee.*

For a moment I forget where I am and chance a glance around the broken-down wall of pillows, most of which are now scattered on the floor beside the bed where they had likely toppled over during the night. Logan's side of the bed is empty and pristinely made so it looks like the sheets have been pressed and never slept in. Throwing off the covers I get to my feet, planning to cross the room to the window, to see who I need to string up for the unnecessary banging at this ungodly hour. Eight AM should be for silence and caffeine consumption exclusively.

I consider shrugging on Logan's robe that is slung over the end of the bed, but resist, opting instead to throw on my old band hoodie in desperate need of a good wash. Sleeping in his bed and swathed in his scent is enough of an intrusion, I don't need to add stealing his clothes to my list of infractions. Pulling the sleeves of my jumper down over my hands, to stave off the trickle of winter air that is circulating in through the weathered mouldings of the single pane glass windows. I glance down into the back garden and almost gasp at the sight. The stark white backdrop of the snow-covered grass, the frost-bitten trees and the milky grey sky is a blank canvas for Logan, his jet-black hair messily swept back, puffs of white clouds falling from his lips at his exertion. Unable to stop staring I allow myself a moment to appreciate every inch of him as he's distracted with the task at hand. Wearing a pair of tattered denim jeans, the cuffs tucked into his signature black army boots, I realise Logan looks good in everything he wears, *or doesn't wear*, I remind myself, remembering him in just a towel yesterday, water droplets running down his torso, a path I wouldn't much mind making with my tongue.

Taking a moment to fill his lungs with the bitter morning air he shrugs out of his navy padded winter coat with the fur trim hood, draping it over a nearby tree stump. I swallow back the lump forming in my throat, aware that once again this man has ruined yet another one of my thongs and he hasn't even touched me. I rub my thighs together as the slick arousal dampens my core. The material of the black vest he's wearing is obscenely tight over his rippling muscles as he bounds across the garden with slats of cherry red wood resting on his shoulder, a hammer held in his other hand. His tan skin covered with predominantly black and grey tattoos makes Logan look more like he belongs to some motorcycle gang, rather than in his position as Lieutenant in the British Armed forces. This man is a chameleon.

'Good with his hands' my brain notes as that familiar snap of interest coils low in my belly. My little Logan-List seems to be growing exponentially the more time I spend with him.

I wanted the treehouse fixed, I hadn't in my wildest dreams considered the possibility that Logan would spend his Christmas Eve taking on the task.

'But boy does he look good doing it.' Got to love my brain for stating the fucking obvious. I watch intently as Logan rolls his shoulders, likely working out a knot in his muscles from all the hammering, using the back of his gloved hand to wipe away the perspiration on his forehead. This man looks all kinds of edible right now and as he turns in my direction, I shift my stance and hide behind the voile curtains, knowing they likely do nothing to hide me from his view. The creak of wood beneath boots pulls my attention back to him as he climbs the board steps nailed into the bark that he has clearly already fixed, as he hauls the slats of wood up into the treehouse. I don't so much mind the banging anymore as he works to stabilise it from the inside, the only downfall now is I can't watch him work. Logan's rippling muscles are far more addictive than the coffee that my body was screaming out for moments ago.

LOGAN

I try to convince myself I'm fixing up the treehouse for the boys, that they should get to enjoy it just as we had as kids, that it would be a shame to have it destroyed after all these years. But every single one of those excuses is a barefaced lie. I'm fixing it because when Candice mentioned our father's plans to tear it down yesterday, Mia looked heartbroken. The expression fleeting and missable to most, burrowed its way into my heart, like so much about that girl does. I knew the only way to make it better, to soothe her in a way I craved to, was to get to work and fix the issue. This is how I found myself out here at the crack of dawn with a hammer and nails in hand as I began repairing a piece of our childhood that *My* Bunny clearly loves.

Should I be doing this? Probably not, not for my reasoning anyway. Memories of the last time I had Mia up in the treehouse, the day I almost kissed her, flit across my mind as I lug another three lengths of wood up the crudely positioned slatted steps. If the torment filling me from her rejection doesn't kill me off, the shitty construction of these steps and the inevitable broken neck when I fall to the ground will. My father is many things, a carpenter is not one of them. I'm surprised the treehouse has lasted this long.

My back straightens, my muscles flexing when I catch Mia watching me from my bedroom window out of my peripheral. Chuckling under my breath as the portable radio churns out *Puddle of Mudd's 'She hates me'*, I edge the line of peacocking for my audience of one, I slip off my winter coat, ensuring she gets an eyeful. Being here at the cabin is the perfect amount of torture, I want her, have done for years, it was so hard to turn my back on her after what happened with Trevor, but I wouldn't stay where I wasn't wanted, and she had made it abundantly clear that there was no space in her life for me anymore. Which is why this is all so confusing, I know I affect her, and it isn't hate or indifference squirrelled away in her expression. There's a part of me now that is questioning everything that happened that night. Being trapped here, unable to leave, I think there might be something between us that she's just not ready to acknowledge. She can deny it all she wants, but I see the way she looks at me when she gets lost in thought. That kiss yesterday was so much more than I think either of us had expected. *My* Bunny is far from the innocent nineteen-year-old I had tried to protect all those years ago.

Memories of the letter she had sent me after that night slices through the joy I had felt moments ago knowing she's up in my bed. Looking at Mia this morning after I had showered, her shapely body buried beneath the covers, the serenity on her beauteous face, the coils of dark red hair splayed out across the white cotton sheets, it was hard not to wake her up and profess my love for her there and then. With the pillow I had slept on tucked in against her chest and pressed up beneath her nose, looking as innocent as she had the day she asked me to kiss her in the tree house, I couldn't imagine the level of hate and disgust written in that letter to even exist in her. She had warned me away, demanding I leave her alone for good, adamant that she never had feelings for me, because *'who could ever fall for a whore of a man who sleeps with any woman that can't escape fast enough'*. To think that that's what she thought of me opens up the old wound in my chest and my heart sinks. The fresh tearing in my soul feeling just as painful as it did the day I opened that damn envelope. Being here at the cabin with her, I'm suddenly questioning everything, because the smile I see here, the smile she seems to save for my eyes only, there is nothing but desire, need and passion there.

I chase away the negative thoughts from three years ago with images of her smiling across the dining table at me, of her wide eyes when I caught her checking out the wrapped present with my nickname for her scrawled on the tag. I fill my head with every picture of her that I can conjure and sigh a heavy breath of relief as the broken parts of me slowly piece themselves back together, *My* Bunny has no idea the power she wields over me, or my heart.

CHAPTER
Eleven

MIA

With the boys tucked up in bed and sound asleep, the tinkling of their Beethoven music box fitted with a starry sky effect light show projecting onto the ceiling, the room is a haven of calm and comfort. With their reindeer themed PJs and their side swept 1940's inspired post bath time hairdo's, they look the epitome of innocent. You'd never have thought they would have been the instigators in the battle Royale spaghetti bolognaise food fight we had endured during dinner. I partly blame Logan for cheering them on and for the slice of garlic bread that ended up wound in my hair. *Big kid,* yet another enticing descriptor to add to my Logan list. The more time I spend with him and after what transpired in the living room yesterday, the more I question what actually happened all those years ago. When he had turned to face me that night, Trevor bloody and spluttering at his feet, I had seen red, shoving Logan out of the way to fall to my knees and tend to Trevor, the Bunny suit the only thing adding a touch of whimsy to the shit show of a situation that had the DJ the music, all the eyes in the room now on our heated car crash appeal exchange.

Before my brain can snap back to the memory, that still to this day fills me with dread, I shake it away, following Candice out of the twin's room stealthily like a ninja on the prowl. When a floorboard creaks under my foot I still, watching with wide eyes as Candice whips soundlessly on the spot, double checking the room behind me to ensure I hadn't fucked up the two hours of prep work that it had taken to get the boys to finally go to sleep. With the coast clear as soft rumbles of a deep sleep fall from their slightly parted lips we creep over the threshold, closing the door carefully behind us like we are handling a bomb.

'Wine, downstairs, games, now' Candice orders as I simply nod my response hightailing it down the carpeted stairs, almost barreling into the front door in the foyer when I misjudge the last step.

'Easy now Bunny,' Logan croons as he cradles me to his broad silencing muscular chest, our bodies dipped at an angle as though someone has pressed pause on the moment our bodies met. That familiar thrum of liquid lust from earlier begins to surge through my veins.

'Wine, downstairs, games, now' I repeat Candice's words with authority, seemingly unable to find any words of my own as the little voice in my head tries to list off all the reasons why grappling Logan around the neck and kissing him again would be a perfectly acceptable second move in a situation such as this. My Knight in sexy cargo pants with the devilish grin and the hooded muddy green eyes also seems to ponder our current position as his grip on my waist tightens.

'*Down Girl*' I bark wordlessly as my core twinges, the mechanics of my arousal kicking into gear with an uncomfortable thud, it had been so long since Trevor had even turned me on that these two days with Logan has whipped my body up into a confused frenzy, making me realise I might not have packed enough underwear. Logan clears his throat, obviously smug that I haven't yet made an attempt to break away from him. Patting down my clothes I do exactly that, welcoming the rush of air not tainted with his intoxicating musk and woodsy scent, only noticing now that he has changed into a crisp white t-shirt free of the tomato sauce stains from dinner, when Candice had a direct hit with a meatball to his chest.

'I've opened the wine, you are downstairs, we of course have games and lastly, I'm not hating that domineering tone Mia.' He beams down at me and my heart shudders in my chest. An unfamiliar longing attached to the jolt of activity. The reaction isn't to something Logan had said but rather something he hadn't. I don't think he has referred to me as anything other than Bunny since he showed up yesterday, yes, he's doing it to tease me, but I actually think it has grown on me, something just the two of us share.

Shit, am I really sad that my best friend's big brother didn't just pet name me?

'*Yes, yes you are*' My brain offers unhelpfully with a chuckle.

I can feel the mist of embarrassment colour my chest, rising up my neck and over my skin until it's crawling across my cheeks. Why is it I wear my emotions so openly with this man? Logan shifts, his hand moving mid-air towards my face, a mixture of concern and intrigue morphing his features as his gaze stays glued to my beetroot-esque face. He knows he's affected me, I'm sure of it.

'Sooo, are we playing?' Randy guffaws as he hangs his head around the living room doorway, snapping Logan and I out of whatever it was that had made these past ten seconds feel like ten minutes. Candice harrumphs with annoyance as she stamps her foot like a child, hitting Randy around the back of the head to chastise him for his interruption, of what could possibly have been a pivotal moment in the little love story Candice believes is inevitable.

'What the hell was that for?' He cries out, rubbing at his head and turning to follow his wife dutifully as she slinks past him.

'Thanks,' I say softly, finally finding my voice. I was grateful for the catch, for the playful exchange, for the heat he stirred in me, but I don't elaborate more than the simple *thanks*. The glint of mirth shining in his eyes tells me that on some level, he already knows, but I appreciate it when he doesn't continue to torture me.

'Gentleman', another word for the mental list where this guy is concerned.

He strolls into the living room and grabs Randy into a headlock, relieving him of the open beer bottle he has and taking a swig. I unapologetically watch him retreat; my stare fixed on the bunched muscles of his shoulders and that pert backside of his that I'd happily drop to my knees and sink my teeth into. *Situation permitting of course.* My lower lip is tugged between my teeth as I stifle a cheeky grin.

'He's also playful' I note, whispering the words aloud with an unchecked smile this time. If he was going to carry on like this, I might have to invest in a notebook and pen.

CHAPTER Twelve

LOGAN

I down the offered shot of Tequila, my fourth if my numbers are correct, with the copious amounts of whiskey and mulled wine in my system I can't be a hundred percent sure. It's hard to keep track when the personification of my wildest dreams is sitting on the floor across from me, our bodies separated by the low coffee table. She hums along with *Jessie J's 'Man with the bag'* that plays through the overhead speakers, lost in thought with a spaced-out expression as she sucks on the nearly completely worn-down candy cane between her lips. I allow my gaze to linger with her distracted. It's the small things that scream the loudest with this woman. The crinkle of her skin around her eyes when she is laughing so hard tears well on her lash line. How animated her hand gestures are when she is telling a story. The way she bites down on her lower lip when she doesn't think I can see her watching me. I fiddle with the dog tags around my neck, the smooth metal between my fingers reminiscent of the cool softness of her skin. Yesterday had been everything I could ever have hoped it

would be, to have her wrapped around me, not an inch of space between us as I devoured her lips on the living room floor. I shudder at the memory, grateful that the coffee table is hiding my lower half, my cock on the brink of pain in its confines as it hardens against my zipper.

Reaching over for Candice's phone from off the table I punch in the code and open up the music app, swiping through the festive playlist until I find what I'm looking for. Like a hit of smelling salts *Eartha Kitt's 'Santa Baby'* begins to play and Mia is sucked back into the present, the haze of zoning out dissipating when her beautiful cerulean eyes meet mine. I know she remembers; I see the workings of the memory flash across her expression, blink and I would have missed it, but I would bet big money on the fact that my little Bunny knows exactly what I'm doing. She breaks the connection and continues to fiddle with her own phone, busying her fingers, I don't know if she even realises, she is silently mouthing along with the lyrics.

I don't know how much longer I can hold out where Mia is concerned. Initially I teased her because I loved her playful comebacks, I longed for the sparkle in those sea-water blue eyes when we were close, but something has shifted, and it is impossible to ignore the rumblings of need that are swimming around in my body now. I don't know what would have happened if Randy hadn't have interrupted us earlier, but I can't deny, if it had been two minutes later, he probably would have got a show the likes of some underground foreign sex extravaganza as I splayed her legs wide on the stairs and got my fill of her right there in the hallway.

Binding her wrists with tinsel behind her back, laying her out across the dining room table, losing myself as our naked bodies writhed with pleasure, undulating over and over again as I pushed her over the edge of complete obliteration repeatedly, making her body sing until she was rung out and on the verge of exhaustion. Hands, mouths, adoration in its purest form. Oh Bunny, how fucking sweet you would look.

'Earth to Logan, you're up.' My sister chimes in, boisterously punching me in the shoulder and dragging me out of my daydream. I consider rising from the floor cushion, throwing Mia over my shoulder, and tugging a length of tinsel from the tree before retreating to my bedroom, but quickly decide against it. I can see I affect her, but I'm not foolish enough to rush this just yet.

I'm about to say dare when I catch a glimpse of my sister's wicked expression. If I say dare she is going to ask me to tell everyone around this table how I really feel about *My* Bunny, and that's something I would like to say to Mia directly, preferably when we are alone and I am balls deep inside her after giving her four orgasms in quick succession. I figure a truth is my safer option, there's ways of getting around that one.

'Truth, little sis.' Any confidence I had fizzles away on a harried breath. I waver, and my smile falls when her grin remains. I'm not entirely sure just yet how I've fucked up, but knowing my little sister as well as I do, I recognise the bloom of triumph in her flawless face.

'What happened the night of your birthday party? What was said to make you hit Trevor?' The colour drains from my face as I glance Mia's way, the air in the room suddenly devoid of the light-heartedness from

82

only moments ago is now heavy with the reminder of a moment in history I'd rather forget entirely. 'She deserves to know, and it should come from you.' My sister presses as she downs a shot of tequila, her penance for snuffing out the perfectly great evening we had been having. Last week my mother had blurted the truth of that night to my sister, swearing her to secrecy until she spoke to me about it. My sister waited all of three minutes yesterday morning to interrogate me when she found me on the sofa beneath the overgrown fur balls Bob and Ross. I made her promise to let me tell Mia myself when the time was right, she clearly thinks I need prompting and that the perfect time is right now during a game of truth or dare.

I want to look at Mia, I want to tell her what is going on, but she just looks hurt, and I know that what I'm going to tell her will only add to that. I silently beg to rewind the clock, to watch her smile so effortlessly again. I had tried to pour out the details of that night in a letter to Mia shortly after it all blew up, but her response convinced me to draw a line in the matter completely, to forget what might have been forming between us, being deployed offered me an out of sight out of mind mentality that I was thankful for, until this weekend anyway, now everything feels different.

CHAPTER Thirteen

LOGAN

3 YEARS EARLIER

W e need more Tequila boss,' my teammate Jackson yells into my ear, *Creep by Radiohead* drowning out his voice a little as it booms out of the floor to ceiling industrial event speakers beside us.

'On it,' I mouth back with a thumbs up, watching as he quickly retreats back to the beer pong table with the group of beautiful women dressed as the *Spice Girls* surrounding it. He promptly has his tongue tangling with the one donning a leopard print dress, with his arm wrapped around the waist of the one sporting pigtails, whilst the one head to toe in sportswear, that I recognise as his ex-girlfriend, scowls at him from the makeshift bar. He is the personification of Thor with his natural shoulder length blond hair, tanned abs, the lightweight silver hammer is a new addition, but his choice of outfit tonight was an easy

decision. The less clothes he had to remove when he got a girl to agree to go home with him was Jackson's MO.

Moving through the crowd, I'm pulled into hugs as people wish me a happy birthday. There was nothing particularly special about turning twenty-three, but this will be the last party for a while whilst I'm stationed overseas, so I'm going to enjoy the night.

I take the steep stairs down to the basement carefully, I might not be drunk, but I can admit my vision is already a little hazy around the edges, so I'm well on my way, and a broken neck is not how I plan on ending this evening. I don't let my mind wander to a certain cute red head dressed head to toe in pink fur upstairs. I'm not allowed to want Mia Grayson. She's my sister's best friend for fucks sake.

 Pulling on the string attached to the overhead bare bulb the bright yellow light chases away the shadows and rather than a stack of alcohol crates and metal beer barrels, I find Trevor with his boxers around his ankles, his bare arse on show as he thrusts like an overworked mechanical bull up inside an intoxicated woman, that from this angle, looks like an extra from the *Gremlins* movie, her ruby red lipstick smeared across her face and his.

I bolt up the stairs, sans the Tequila I had been looking for, in search of Mia, I will try to swallow down the judgement that will likely want to escape my lips when I find her, because I had tried to warn her off Trevor, numerous times. As I scan the room for bunny ears, I remind myself to keep my shit together, hitting her with an *I told you so* isn't how I need to play this, she's already going to be devastated, I don't need to make this worse. Instead of finding Mia's beautiful face I find his as he storms through the dancing guests between us. I can't help but laugh in the fuckers' face, only a moron would risk what he has.

'You have it all, you have Mia and you're back there, diddlying with second best, why?'

'Ever tried to fuck a virgin?'

I'm stunned by the question, a little hopeful that he is speaking about Mia, because I can't imagine her as anything but pure, especially at the hands of this dickhead.

'A man has needs, she ain't cutting it. I put in the effort and time, and still nothing,'

'She loves you,' I hate the words the second they slip from my mouth, but I know they are true, I've overheard Candice and Mia talking, she is in love with this prick, and I don't know what magical powers he possesses but my usually suspicious sister seems to love him too. This guy should list acting as his major.

'You can make this right. I don't see why you should exactly, this current situation being a massive red flag, but she loves you.' I add, that last tagged on truth feeling like gritty sand in my mouth. This would destroy Mia, especially after how hard she fought for us to accept him.

'I love to fuck, warming up a girl past friend status is exhausting. I've been working for two months to get inside that tight little body, probably a fucking exquisite cunt, if she'd let me have a taste.'

I've punched the fucker before he even got his last word out, breathing heavily as my shoulders shake, rage filling my veins like a shot of adrenaline. I want to fucking obliterate him, but my head is playing catchup, I've reacted before my sense of composure has a minute to assess the situation. I block out the rumblings of the interested crowd that has formed around us when he swipes at my legs and bucks me off his chest right before I'm about to land another blow to his face. Standing at full height he winces and bows as the punch I levelled with his gut radiates pain throughout his torso. He spits a mouthful of blood at my feet on the black and white chequered dance floor, a wicked grin etched across his features, as I hear Mia demanding people move out of her way as she shuffles through the crowd towards us. She sees me before she sees him and rushes to my side, I look down at her, an apology heavy in my gaze and she appears confused when she seemingly recognises the silent sentiment.

'Logan, what happened,' she worries, reaching up to trace the bloody split in my lip, the lucky shot Trevor got in before pushing me away.

'He's a maniac,' I hear Trevor growl out from behind her, his slumped form shaking with heavy breaths. I see the grotesque mask of pain contort his features and I know instantly that he is going to milk this for everything he can. The heat from her touch disappears when she turns to cradle his body. Those enthralling doe eyes of hers like saucers as panic constricts her vocal cords.

'Oh my God Trevor, what happened?' she cries out, pulling him over to a nearby bench.

Turning on me with a feral anger creeping across her features she blows out a frustrated breath.

'I don't know what this is about, but did you really have to hit him?' I don't answer her question right away because my gaze is trained on the smirking bag of shit that is pawing at his wounds behind her. She shoves me in my chest to get my attention, which does nothing to move me considering the vast differences in our heights and weights.

'I know you don't like him; you've made that abundantly clear Logan, but I love him, you said you understood. You said you would try,'

'I lied,' I spit out, wanting desperately to pick her up in my arms and kiss the anger right out of her. After numerous hour long conversations at my parents after she initially told me she was hooking up with my mortal enemy, I had conceded and dropped the issue, mainly because I thought it would work itself out and he would either get bored or she would come to her senses, sadly neither of those occurred, hence why I find myself here with bloody knuckles and oddly aroused by this redheaded temptress who currently looks like she wants to gut me.

'Seems like lying is your thing, doesn't it Logan.' She wipes away a tear that is threatening to fall from the corner of her eye and I'm questioning whether that show of sadness is for me or him. She turns on her heels and when she's almost to him, I find my voice.

'Bunny,' I yell, unable to get out the real reason why I was pounding on her good for nothing boyfriend's face, but she holds up a hand to silence me. With trembling lips and sorrow clouding her usually bright blue eyes she turns back to face me, while laying a reassuring hand on Trevor's shoulder. I can't deny that her little show of taking his side feels like a *Muhammad Ali* worthy punch to my chest.

'I thought we could be friends, I once even stupidly thought....' She cuts herself off, looking around at our audience, as though she is suddenly realising we're not alone. When I move forward, intent on asking her to finish her sentence, she hits me with the knockout blow.

'Don't call me, don't talk to me, just don't Logan. I don't have enough energy to keep having this conversation. I'm done.' She softly retorts, each word holding a weight that threatens to smother me for good. I watch her leave, the truth of what happened dying on my tongue the further into the room she gets. I've lost her. I don't deserve the likes of Mia, I never have, and I likely never will. Guys like me don't win in situations like this. I'll give her time, a couple of days at least to calm down and then I will tell her everything, not because I want her for myself but because I care for her and her happiness. I may not deserve her but neither does Trevor.

CHAPTER Fourteen

MIA

PRESENT DAY

I am seething when he climbs the narrow wooden slats up to meet me in the treehouse. Pacing the eight-foot by eight-foot space is comical, there isn't enough room to swing a cat in here, but my frustration refuses to acknowledge the comedic value of such irony. I'm angry, blood boiling, finger twitching angry. How could he not tell me the truth? How could he let me spend three years with Trevor? I realise quickly as I strip off my padded winter jacket, desperate for the frigid night air to nip at my skin until I can't feel anything else but the burn of the unrelenting elements, that I'm asking the wrong questions. What I really want to know is why didn't he take me, claim me, own me. Because if I'm being honest with myself, it was always about Logan. I realise now, I was never hurt because he hit Trevor, I was hurt because he didn't demand I be his. I wouldn't let myself see the truth because I felt undeserving of his attention.

'You lied to me' I spit out, unable to correlate thought with speech as I continue to frantically pace in the small space.

'I didn't lie, I gave you a couple of days to cool off and then I told you everything and you turned me away. You think I wanted that night to turn out the way it did?' He bellows, watching me as I continue to wear the wood beneath my feet.

'BUNNY!' Logan snaps, grabbing onto my arms and stopping me in my tracks. The lack of light only proves to intensify his darkened gaze as the moon casts a shadow down over his features, his black hair falling forward over his forehead.

'I know you are upset right now, but I did what I did that night for you. I wanted you to be mine, I always wanted you.' He barks through clenched teeth as he releases me, as though he's only now realising what he has said. My mouth agape, I immediately miss the warmth of his touch on my bare arms.

'When you blocked me from your phone, your messenger, your email, I had to resort to more archaic methods,' he adds, pushing his hair back into place, his hand lingering at the nape of his neck.

'What the fuck does that mean?' I bite back, my brain unhelpfully offering up morse code as an explanation, an attempt to bring some levity to this shit show of an interaction. It is certainly not the time for my witty one-woman inner monologue.

'It means Bunny, when you cut me out of your life I sent you a letter, an honest to God handwritten profession of everything that happened that night and exactly how I felt about you. Don't play dumb Mia, please.' A mixture of terseness and hurt pinches at his vocal cords and I immediately want to calm him, but I don't, instead I keep my distance, or as much as this small space will allow.

'I….I..' I can't seem to express what I want to say as I gulp like a fish fresh out of water.

'You're telling me you have no idea what I'm talking about?' He utters disbelievingly as his brows knit in confusion, intently searching my taut expression for the truth he believes I'm hiding from him.

I shake my head in response because right now I seem to have forgotten every word in the English language. He sent me a letter and I apparently responded. It occurs to me suddenly, as I stare into his wide sparkling green eyes masked almost entirely by the shadows of the starless night sky, that I have spent three years missing some key information. Trevor had clearly intercepted Logan's letter and responded for me, I wonder now how much of our relationship was ever real, because you don't screw with someone you profess to love like he had. Refusing to allow that man a moment more of my headspace, I take a breath and resign myself to leaving it all in the past where it belongs. Swiftly the energy in the room changes and it's clear I don't need to say another word. I need to show Logan exactly how I feel, how I've always felt.

I lunge forward, jumping up and wrapping my legs around his waist, pinning him against the exposed tree trunk that winds in through the four walls of the miniature house. He grunts as his back connects with the rough bark, but he doesn't push me off of him. Instead, he tightens his grip and runs a hand up into my hair, tugging harshly so pin pricks of pain spread across my scalp. I go gooey in his embrace, desperate for him to enact his own brand of torture worship on my body until pain becomes so intrinsically mixed with pleasure that I no longer know where he begins, and I end. Everything this man has to offer me, I want it all, every drugging lap of his tongue against my skin threatens to push me over the edge as he hungrily nips his way up my throat like I'm the only source of sustenance he needs to survive.

The assault of the harsh bite of the frigid elements against my heated skin dissipates, our bodies entwined as I grip onto him like he might disappear if I let go. My hands grapple to explore every inch of his body as I writhe in his hold and take his mouth with mine, tongues warring as I finally get my fill of Logan Sinclair.

'Fuck..' Logan barks when I roll my hips, my slick centre pressing against his hardening cock through his trousers. He holds me with one hand under my backside to shake off his winter coat, changing his position to get his other arm free as he dots featherlight kisses along my jawline. I pull my top up over my head, grateful I opted to go without a bra after my shower. My nipples harden under his perusal as his jaw slackens and his hooded gaze drinks me in.

'You should be shirtless always,' he mumbles flicking his tongue over my peaked nipple, biting down gently when goosebumps skitter across my chest. The softness of his adoration of my body is largely conflicted with the harshness of his grip on my lower half. It takes me a second to realise he has already snapped open the clasp on my jeans as he pushes his hand beneath the material of my underwear, pressing me against the wall with his weight as he plunges two fingers between my folds with a guttural roar without warning, a punishing move that has me clenching around the intrusion as my body welcomes him there. Joined in a way I had wished for but had never allowed myself to believe could ever come true.

'Logan, fuck, shit….' My head snaps back and I embed my nails into the nape of his neck, my legs shaking as the ghost of his satisfied smile imprints itself into the crook my neck. His movements are torturously slow, and a needy whimper falls from my shaking lips when he spreads his fingers a little inside me, the heel of his hand applying pressure exactly where I need it for me to discover the spiralling tendrils of my building high.

'You want more Bunny?' He teases.

'Please,' I beg, pulling back as much as our entwined bodies will allow so I can get a better look at the handsome face I've dreamt about for countless nights over the years. Even with his fingers buried inside me there is an unspoken question that lingers between us, the moment is too big for such a small space and we both understand that we are crossing a line we will likely never be able to walk away from.

'I need you Logan, I need all of you, please don't make me beg,'

'But you look so fucking beautiful when you beg me, Bunny,' he whispers tauntingly with a wide grin.

'In that case, pretty please ruin me for all other men Soldier Boy, I need this,'

He doesn't need to respond with words, the spark of fire that lights in his eyes is response enough. Adding a third finger, his free hand gripping onto my arse hard enough to leave marks he doesn't hesitate to curl his fingers up inside me, the heel of his hand no longer tentative as he roughly massages my clit. It's too much and not enough all at once and as the precipice of my release crests over my senses I welcome the fragility in my weakened state. Feeling protected, adored, and desired in his strong arms.

'Yes, Oh, shit, Logan, don't stop,' I whine, encouraging him to continue as white spots dance behind my closed eye lids. Gripping onto the collar of his t-shirt to the point my knuckles are white the fabric tears like tissue paper under the strain, with his rock-hard abs exposed, the tinkling of his dog tags cold against my fingertips, I tighten my thighs around his waist, a slave to the way he is pleasuring my body, each thrust of his hand determined as I clench around him. His wide stance holding me up, so I feel weightless.

'I should have claimed you all those years ago, I should have been your first everything, but if you'll let me, I promise to own and worship every one of your lasts,' The sentiment is too much, too much like love that it causes a rush of fear to settle in my belly, the realisation that from here on out, nothing will ever be the same again between us. I don't want to know what an after without him might look like. Claiming my mouth, he uses his knees to spread my legs wider, hitting inside me at a new angle that has me crying out, spluttered bursts of my heavy breaths visible in the bitter air as I bite down on my lip, the coppery tang of blood coating my tongue.

'Fuck Bunny, do you know what you do to me?'

I can feel the heat of his stare against my skin, but I'm too far gone to answer his question or meet his gaze. He watches me intently as the most powerful orgasm I've ever felt rockets through my body, every nerve tingling with overwhelming sensations as I pant through it, my heart clawing against my rib cage as I plummet into the choppy waters of utter bliss. I stay connected to him as I slump forward, resting my forehead against his shoulder as lazy aftershocks of heat zing through my extremities. He holds me protectively against his burly form, allowing me the time I need to come down from my high as he pulls his hand out of my jeans. I miss the feeling of fullness almost immediately.

Readjusting me against him he gently drops me onto my unsteady feet, making sure to keep the connection between us as he grips onto the back of my neck, running his nose up and over my pulse points into my hair to inhale a lungful of my scent. My vision cloudy, I follow the movement as he stands to his full height. He pushes the fingers one at a time that he had inside me between his full lips, cleaning me from them, humming his approval as he pulls each one free with a slick *pop*.

'The sweetest taste,' He adds, tightening his grip as I whimper, and my knees threaten to give way.

'Logan' I begin, not entirely clear on what my response will be.

'Interrupting something am I?' Candice yells up at us from down in the garden.

'We decided to take you up on that clue you wanted to gift us for Christmas,' I yell down and watch with amusement as the pieces fall into place for Logan.

'You heard me talking to Candice in my room? You were there?'

'Hiding under the bed, you owe me a new thong.' I chuckle with a raised brow, remembering his little show in the shower that had me climaxing in my shorts yesterday.

'I plan to dirty you up way worse than I did your underwear, so unless I can start a tab this could get pricey. I plan on destroying a fair few items from your underwear collection, pre warning Bunny.'

'I've been all for this union for years guys,' Candice adds, 'but please for the love of all that's holy, can we keep the cringy sex talk between yourselves for when I'm out of earshot?'

Dropping to the rug on the floor by the entryway, I shuffle over to the edge and hang my head over the wooden ledge, peering down at my friend with a goofy grin on my face. Standing and leaning out of the treehouse doesn't seem like the best idea right now considering my head is still swimming with what has just transpired. Candice stands in at least a foot of snow and frosted flakes continue to fall from the sky. Three sets of tracks leading out from the house are the only disturbance in the blanket of white that covers the acres of land surrounding the cabin.

'If you didn't want to hear our conversation you should have left little Sis,' Logan yells out from behind me.

'The tree was practically swaying at the roots, I was concerned for the conservation of the wildlife,' she beams up at me. 'Now it's cold and this is freeze your tits off weather, you may be fucking my brother but I'm your friend and I can still be concerned for your welfare.'

'Being nosey is not an extension of friendship goals.' I state.

'Big words for a brother fucker,' she chuckles, and I can't help but laugh heartily along with her.

'Is this a thing, do you ladies want me to leave?' Logan grumbles as he joins me on the ledge, propped up by his elbow as he rests his fist against his temple, zero care of what Candice can see when I run my finger over the torn fabric of his top that is on show. He gazes down at his sister who is bundled up for the artic weather, the heat of arousal I will forever more consider reserved for my eyes only lighting his features. I enjoy the desire currently warming my blood knowing I can have as much of Logan as I want now. He traces invisible swirls up the curve of my spine without thinking and I have to shove away that lingering spark of interest that has me wanting to straddle him and ride him into next week audience be damned. *Poor Candice* My brain offers and I'm inclined to agree, Candice doesn't deserve to be scarred with the memory of me chasing my orgasm while her brother is balls deep inside of me.

'I'm happy for you two, but I'm sure as shit not looking after you both when you wake up with hypothermia tomorrow. I have the twins to keep me enough busy.'

'Love you,' I cajole as we watch her retreat into the house with a wave.

'She isn't wrong, I don't want to gain an epic finger blasting experience with a hot as fuck soldier on the same night I potentially lose all feeling in my toes. Hypothermia is no joke.'

'I've been staving off a crippling bout of sexual tension for the past three years, I'm ready to tough out the elements for as long as you need me to little Bunny.'

———————

Getting everything back in place, the searing heat burned into my skin from his touch still present, I follow close behind him as he takes my hand in his and leads me up to his room.

The house is quiet and every step we take up the winding staircase sounds thunderous. I should be questioning what we are doing, I should be dutifully reminding myself of all the reasons why I shouldn't be following him upstairs, all the cons as to why this will never work out for us. But my brain refuses to jump past the drumming thrill of utter elation I felt in the treehouse when he had his hand between my thighs. The memory of our union coats my skin like a comforting blanket and my greedy libido wants more, as though a living breathing entity after all this time of pining after a man she thought she could never call hers, she wants everything Logan has to offer and she's not about to let a sane thought distract her. Tonight, she would bask in the Christmas miracle she has been dreaming about since she was fourteen years old, although a kiss on the cheek that teenage Mia had hoped for is a far cry from what grown Mia plans on taking from Logan tonight, with age her desires have changed some.

CHAPTER
Fifteen

MIA

W hat you said last night, about your cameras?' I say sweetly, pulling my lower lip between my teeth as I try to spot in the room where they would be hidden, slightly nervous incase Logan thinks I'm absolutely crazy.

'I have them, but the moment I saw you were in here, I turned them off, felt like an invasion of privacy and I'm nothing if not a gentleman.'

'You want my permission Soldier boy?' I say loftily as I lower to my knees on the plush carpet between his legs.

'You want to know if I would like to film us fucking? Homemade porn feels like a fitting gift this festive season Bunny,'

'I have thought about what it would feel like to have you inside me Logan since that night I planned on kissing you in the treehouse, it would be a shame not to immortalise it,' I almost don't recognise my own lust-laden voice as I lay out exactly what I'm thinking before my brain has a chance to filter it. 'You on board?' I giggle, throwing caution

to the wind as I start to unbutton the shirt he threw on when we came upstairs, slow enough so he has a chance to stop me if he wants to.

He groans with a broad grin etched across his lips as he runs a hand through his slightly damp hair, my fingers skimming his chiselled torso as I make it down to the belt buckle of his jeans. Gazing up into his mottled green irises rimmed with a warm amber he silently urges me to continue. Pulling out his phone he swipes the screen and opens the app that controls the cameras. I hear the quiet chime from somewhere in the room but there isn't any indication as to where they are hidden.

Caressing my cheek with his thumb, Logan takes hold of my chin, directing me to look first above us at the fan with the attached Edison bulb light feature, the hidden lens tucked away in the mouldings. He then moves my face towards the faux potted plant on his dresser drawers near the bathroom, which has a perfect side view of his bed and the mirrored wardrobe doors beyond it. Heat fizzles at my core as he pulls my face back around to meet his heated gaze.

'All the angles covered,' He grins, lowering his fingers from my chin and I whimper in response, hating the loss of his touch, now that I know how good it feels.

LOGAN

I look down at the woman I would happily die a thousand deaths for, losing my mind as she works the buttons of my shirt open, her fingers grazing against my tattooed skin as she leisurely makes her way down to my belt buckle. I only threw it on when we came upstairs so I could watch her eyes widen with interest the way they had earlier. Desperate for a glimpse of that sinfully innocent doe expression of hers, a new addiction I welcome. Thoughts of wrapping the leather around her wrists and securing her to my bed frame, as I spend the night feasting on her body, has my cock hardening in my jeans. Not that it takes much with this beauty between my legs. A squeak of understanding as she glances south has a slick grin creeping across my lips, flecks of grey crystallising in her sea-blue-coloured eyes as pride swamps her expression, a spark of realisation filling her as she finally sees the effect she has on me.

'Fuck Bunny, torturing me is the game you really want to play?' I chide, secretly edging her to do exactly that, knowing there will be nothing sweet or reserved about what I will do to her when I take the lead. I'll let her explore for now, there is something magical about the soft gasps of interest that fall from her full lips when she discovers a new dip or curve of my body.

'This has been long overdue,' I brusquely retort, just about ready to throw her down on the bed and take her to the edge until she's begging me for her release.

Mia has an effortless kind of beauty, she's most stunning when she's nervous or frustrated, when her cheeks pink and highlight the smattering of freckles across the bridge of her button nose. She doesn't need makeup or push up bras, she rocks an oversized tee with as much finesse as a classy model walks a runway. It is the moments when she doesn't think I'm looking that I treasure.

Coiling my fingers around a curl of her deep red hair I tug lightly, testing the waters, the amber rimmed glint of mirth circling her irises, and her full bottom lip tugged between her teeth gives me the answer to my unspoken question. Reaching her scalp, I gather a handful at her nape and tug a little more forcefully, angling her head back so I can dip down and kiss her. I greedily swallow the groan of pleasure that tumbles free of her mouth in response. Claiming it as mine.

'I can't wait to hear you scream out my name again,' the husky edge to my tone sounds animalistic.

'What about everyone in the house?'

I love that she hasn't denied that she will scream for me but that she's worried we might wake the others in the house.

'Dad soundproofed this room when I was going through my indie rock band phase, we're good to go Bunny.' I don't add that the single pane window allows for the outside world to hear us, because in the dead of night with the nearest house being five miles away, the only witnesses will be the wildlife. Likely happy with the idea of being able to let loose Mia's expression darkens, the thoughts of what she plans to do to me present in the wicked twist of her full lips. There is a hidden edge to this woman, and I plan on encouraging her at every turn to take what she wants from me, as and when she's ready. Any patience I might have thought I possessed moments ago is obliterated when Mia stands and removes her clothing, her dazed hooded gaze never leaving my face, her nipples peaked under the bite of arctic winter air circling the room.

Her soft skin is almost buttery under the amber glow of the lamp light. She makes me want to be gentle, to adore her the way she deserves, to treat her like a princess. But every sentiment I can think of is knocked on its head when Mia Jane Grayson, the red headed pocket rocket with the smoking hot body and the wicked personality to match, surprises me and leaves me speechless.

'Either you pin me down by my throat Logan and fuck me senseless or you lay down and take what I'm offering. I've been waiting far too long for this, stop treating me like I'm going to break.'

Her order seems to shock even her as that familiar flush of embarrassment colours her skin a peony pink. Clearly my Christmas Bunny has never demanded what she wants before. I put her out of her misery, lifting her feet clean off the floor as I press her into the tartan armchair, sinking to my knees and tearing the lace thong from her body without a second thought.

'One to add to the list of what I owe you,' I smirk, before dipping down and running the pad of my tongue up her centre. Her body rocks in my grasp and I push down on her belly, locking her in place as she calls out my name. Every lap of my tongue and pinch of her clit has her calling out my name, begging me to stop or to continue, it isn't clear. I do know she could rip my hair out at the roots, and I wouldn't stop. I can feel as her release builds when she claws at my tattooed arm that is wrapped around her thigh, holding her open for me when the rush of sensations have her instinctively try to close her legs around my head. When her hands fly up into her hair and her back arches up off the chair, I thrust two thick fingers up inside her, earning the scream I had said I wanted, and it has my cock throbbing painfully in my pants. This right here is the best kind of torture. Keeping the same pace, using my tongue to flick and massage her clit she detonates, her slickness rolling down my fingers and coating my hand. Rising on my haunches I take in my new favourite view as I lazily continue to move inside her, pressing down on her lower belly and prolonging her orgasm.

'Fuuuccckkk meeee,' she stutters out, wiping her sweat speckled forehead as she grins down at me sleepily, every heavy panting breath breaking free from her lips, music to my ears.

'You had enough yet Bunny?' I ask, already knowing the answer by the wanton glint colouring her seawater-blue eyes with flecks of fiery amber. I would happily drown in those eyes of hers.

'Not even close Soldier boy,' she giggles, sitting up and pulling me towards her by my belt buckle.

'Now I need to know how you taste.' She sing-songs airily with a playful arched brow. Pawing at me as though I am the most desirable sweet treat she's ever discovered. This girl is full of surprises it seems. Who am I to deny her.

CHAPTER
Sixteen

MIA

Lust drunk is a new and heady sensation I've never experienced before. With Trevor, getting on my knees for him was something I did to placate him when I wasn't in the mood for sex, a consolation prize so he wouldn't spend the rest of the evening making me feel terrible for not *'meeting his needs like a partner should'*. This, with Logan feels entirely different, I want to make him feel as blissfully spent and adored as he has me. I want to lavish him with sensations that will have him desperate to fill me to the hilt and use my body however he wants. I gaze up at him through my thick lashes, leisurely unbuckling his belt, the ridge of his hardened cock already pressing against its denim confines, begging to be freed.

'I am this close to bending you over my knee and teaching you some time management Bunny,' Logan balks with his thumb and forefinger held out, the sliver of space between them the proof of how much I am torturing him with my slow pace of undressing him. 'I wouldn't be totally against that,' I reply sweetly, snapping open the line of buttons that show me Logan is going commando under his jeans. I appreciate the quick access when I slide them down to his knees and his cock practically throbs under my perusal. For a second, I question the logistics of whether it will actually fit in my mouth considering the sheer girth and length of it. Logan has certainly been blessed in the trouser department.

I'm no quitter, I'll make it fit. I decide quickly.

I drag the flat of my tongue up the slit, lapping at the pre-cum and murmuring my approval, licking my lips, and meeting his heated gaze to further tease him.

'My suspicions were correct, you taste delicious,' I say breathily.

'Oh fuck,' he growls. I pull his hand up and tangle it in my hair, silently nodding my permission for him to be a little rougher with his touch. I know he is trying to take this slow for my benefit, he doesn't want to rush me. But I need him to know that this is what I need, my very own claiming from Logan Sinclair has been top of my naughty Christmas wish list for the past three years. It should always have been him and I. He should have been my first. This is where we make amends.

'Look at you Bunny, the embodiment of perfection, on your knees for me. I am the luckiest fucker to walk the earth.'

I preen at his appraisal, pushing out my chest as I throw caution to the wind and take as much of him as I can manage into my mouth, hollowing out my cheeks and flattening my tongue when I feel the tip of his cock hit the back of my throat. I gag a little as I work my way back and forward, addicted to the appreciative heady sounds rumbling out of his mouth as his fingers tangle in my hair and his hips begin to move. I welcome the painful pinch on my scalp as my core throbs, my little kitty desperate to be filled. Logan pulls me off him with a slick pop, his chest rising and falling as his pupils dilate, a rooted hunger darkening the emerald green I'm used to. He dips down to my level and kisses me with a ferocity that threatens to send me spiralling without him even being inside me. With his swollen lips hovering mere inches from mine, he holds me in place, the fingers of his free hand running up the inside of my thigh and exploring the slick path between my legs.

'I need to be inside you Bunny, I've spent the past three years imagining what you might feel like, how you might bend to my touch, how hot this would be.'

'Take me, take it all, please Logan, show me what I've been missing,' His name is nothing more than a breathless whisper, the desperation I would usually try to hide when around this man heavy in my tone. It's all he needs to hear, his hooded eyes glittering with anticipation as the caged beast inside him is unleashed. He hauls me up into his arms as though I weigh nothing, his meaty palms grabbing a handful of my arse cheeks and raising me until he has my back pinned up against the wall. I expect him to lose control and thrust up into me, the panic of his size clearly filtering into my expression because there is nothing hurried about his next move. The corded muscles of his torso contract as he works against gravity to hold my body in place, the tip of his length teasing my entrance but never plunging in. He's being careful with me. With one hand still supporting me he reaches the other up to my face, his fingers tucking a stray red curl of my hair behind my ear, his tentative touch lingering on my jaw as he beckons my gaze to meet his with a dip of his head.

'We go at your pace, always at your pace.' He assures me. Keeping our eyes fixed I lower myself and slowly impale myself on his rock-hard cock, shuddering as my body struggles to grant his wide girth entry. Heat pools at my filled centre as an uncontrollable fire rages in my belly. It's too much and not enough at the same time. I need him to know this okay, but I can't seem to find the words. I've never been cared for like this, I've never known sex to be so enthralling and passionate.

'Hold on Mia,' Logan says, and I do, gripping onto his broad shoulders with such force that I'm sure my nails will leave indents in his tattooed flesh. He begins to move, thrusting his hips back and forth, a steady rhythm with a pounding, unrelenting melody. I chance a glance between our bodies to see where he is filling me, I'm so impossibly full and the delicious ache vibrating at my core is greedy for more.

'Logan, please,' I beg, and he groans, realising that now I am ready for whatever he has in store for me.

Moving us over to the bed, carrying me as though I weigh nothing, his cock still buried inside me, he begins to fuck me, slipping his hand around my neck and holding me in place against the mattress he thrusts up inside me with abandon, the teasing pressure of his fingers over my pulse points causing the relentless thump of my heart to pound in my ears. The change in position has him hitting a new spot inside me, he feels bigger, harder, thicker. My back arches and a cry of pleasure tumbles from my lips, tipping up my chin with the hand locked around my throat he angles my face to meet his. He bends over me, swallowing down my whimpers as he hits me with a drugging kiss, a kiss so powerful that I know I will forever more be addicted to this man. Every plunge of his hips feels determined as he fills me. I want it all, everything he's willing to give me. My body shudders, my core tightening around his shaft as my head goes light, my vision spotty. Pure unfiltered pleasure sweeps through my veins like a shot of liquid lust as my psyche splinters and I come explosively around him.

I don't have time to recover when Logan grins down at me and says, 'I need another one, I could watch you come apart like that every minute of every day and it still never be enough, Bunny.'

He slows his thrusts a little, warming me back up as the feeling returns to my extremities. He tugs my lower lip between his teeth and bites down, the zinging shock of pain dragging me back to the moment. His fingers trace along the sweat slicked valley down between my breasts, over my belly button and down between our joined bodies. His fingers clamp onto my clit and his thrusts pick up speed. Rolling the sensitive nub between his fingers he roars as his release approaches. Every one of my senses goes into overdrive as I grip onto the taut skin of his shoulders, my own release close enough I can practically taste it. He slams into me three more times, taking us both over the cliff's edge as we chase our orgasms in unison. Shattering on a garbled scream of pure intoxicating pleasure my body goes limp as he collapses on top of me. I revel in the weight of him caging in my oversensitive body, the mingling of our laboured breaths filling the quiet room, the clattering of my heart loud in my ears as I try to find a comfortable rhythm. Logan slips out of me and falls at my side, pulling me in so my back is flush with his chest. His nose explores the soft spot beneath my ear and roams into my mess of wild red curls, inhaling as though my scent is the only thing tethering him to this moment.

'Damn. That was worth waiting three years for. Let's do it again,' Logan cheekily whispers against my shoulder, nipping spiritedly at my skin, and every cell in my body thrums with agreement.

A literal God - I mentally note. Just another thing to add to my Logan list.

CHAPTER
Seventeen

MIA

S tretching my limbs that feel heavy and overworked thanks to the bedroom Olympics I partook in last night with Logan, I pull his pillow to my face, inhaling his natural musk scent as my core throbs. We couldn't get enough of each other and even with only an hour or so of rest, I want more, I need more of him. Reaching out I hate that his side of the bed is so cold and already made in the way that screams military man. I muss up his work, winding my legs around the covers and wrapping myself up like a burrito. I would happily spend the rest of the foreseeable future pinned against his mattress whilst he worships my body. A girl can hope, this is the time for miracles after all.

The faraway beginnings of a Christmas tune plays out from downstairs, the faintest redolence of sizzling bacon wafting into the room as the door is propped open with Logan's battered military issue boots. I should be grateful for the moment to collect myself as he

potters about downstairs in the kitchen, I do need a second to wrap my head around everything that happened last night. I close my eyes and let my thoughts drift, the invisible weight of him laying over me, holding my wrists in one of his hands above my head as he sucks and nips at my neck, pinning me down with his hips as his thick thighs spread me open wide, the delicious ache at my core a welcomed reminder of the best sex of my life.

The sated chuckle rumbles through me as I jump out of his bed and skip over like one of the *Von Trapp* children to grab for his robe, which is slung over the back of the tartan armchair in the corner of the room. Messing with my hair I attempt to arrange it into a messy top knot, pulling free some strands around my face to soften the look, suddenly worrying how I'm meant to hide my stupidly giddy smile from Candice, Randy, and the boys over breakfast. If thoroughly fucked had an expression it would be the one currently slapped on my face. Try as I might, I can't seem to wipe the grin from my lips, and I feel it in the pinch in my cheeks.

Even while brushing my teeth the stupid grin on my face remains. Filling my lungs with a steading breath after rinsing out my mouth I grip onto the marble side and lean my forehead against the mirror. Moving over to the shower I turn the handle and watch as the room quickly fills with steam. I could do with a long soak in a bubble bath to work out the knots in my muscles, but I have a handsome man currently cooking me breakfast, so time is of the essence, a quick shower will have to do. Slipping out of his robe is about as far as I get as the steam from the shower fogs up the mirror, a message that had been invisible now appearing on the glass.

'Follow the candy, Bunny.'

Filled with intrigue I turn off the shower, moving back into his bedroom and grabbing an oversized t-shirt from Logan's wardrobe. Slipping on one of my thongs out of the top drawer of his dresser next, thankfully the t-shirt reaches mid-thigh and covers my arse because that man has ruined all the sleep shorts I had packed. Now I'm ready to play my Soldier Boy's game.

As promised my path downstairs to the kitchen is littered with my favourite sweet treat, hooked onto door handles, resting atop picture frames, tucked away into the holly decorations winding around the banister. This might be the first time in history that I don't need the sugar rush, just the idea of finding Logan at the end of this little treasure hunt is enough to have my pulse spiking and my brain fizzing with excitement.

CHAPTER
Eighteen

MIA

W hen I make it to the kitchen, I have to do a double take. *Mariah Carey's 'All I want for Christmas'* begins to play and I lean against the door frame, getting a good look at the glorious scene playing out in front of me. If there was any doubt that this man could be any cuter, this moment right here, completely obliterates it. Swaying his hips, every taut muscle of his shirtless torso defined, that pronounced V at his waist on show as his dark wash denim jeans hang low around his hips, his feet bare. I lick my lips and settle in for the show. Singing along like a seasoned artist he lays into the tune, his gruff interpretation lighting a fire in my belly as he continues to move the bacon around in the pan, letting it crisp to near complete incineration, just how I like it.

Spinning on his toes, spatula in hand, he finally sees me in the doorway. His face lights up, dimpled cheeks, hooded gaze, a dusting of a five o'clock shadow on his jawline and a broad smile set in place as I get a good look at him. He's wearing white furry bunny ears attached to a Santa hat and a red bow tie around his neck and boy does he look

gorgeous.

'What is festive about Bunnies?' I question, merely filling the silence

with sound as heat pools in my belly and a slickness coats my

underwear, as he removes the pan from the stove. He could be draped

in a bin bag right now and I'd still climb him like a fucking tree.

'The theme felt fitting for us Bunny. You can add a Santa hat to

anything and it makes it festive,' he chuckles, flicking the furry bobble

at the end of his hat.

'I'm not going to argue with that,' I retort, practically dribbling as his

taut torso muscles flex under the overhead honey coloured strip lights

when he reaches up to stretch.

'I'm feeling left out,' I mock pout.

'Lucky for you I got a delivery before the snow hit,' he beams, the

candy cane hanging from the corner of his mouth as he stirs the coffee

he has made for me, decorating it with a squirt of cream and

marshmallows before crossing the kitchen to meet me. Holding it out

and grinning around the sweet treat between his teeth I shudder at the

sight of him, heat coursing through my veins as my fingers itch to feel

his skin. This man affects me on a level beyond normal comprehension,

I'm two minutes shy of selling my soul to Krampus to get us locked in

this magic bubble of a day for the rest of eternity.

I step to the side, my hands tightening around the steaming mug as I

take a sip and groan appreciatively, the needed hit of caffeine soaring

through my deliciously taut muscles, kneading them into submission as

breakfast is forgotten. When he strolls back into the kitchen holding the holly papered gift, I turn to follow his woodsy musk scent as he places it down on the sofa beside the dining table. Relishing the burn on my tongue as I sip my coffee.

I snap out of my daydream, the one that has me considering bolting the doors and windows from the inside, so we never have to ever leave here again, and I ask the question my brain has been silently screaming at me.

'Where is Candice? Randy? The boys?' I feel stupid that it has taken me this long to ask the obvious, but Logan has a way of blind sighting me with his mere proximity.

'They dusted off the sleighs and headed over to mum and dads, is that okay with you little Bunny?'

'Your mum's going to hate me for stealing you away.'

'Mum is over the moon, apparently the Sinclair women have known for years about our potential. In two days she gets to meet my amazing, smart, beautiful new girlfriend. She is probably making a ten-tier celebratory cake as we speak.'

'So, you have a girlfriend, she sounds wonderful,' I tease.

'Yes, I do, and I'm *hopping* mad for her,' he croons as he pulls me in against his shirtless tattooed chest. Relieving me of my coffee and placing the mug down on the table. I theatrically roll my eyes even though that is quite possibly the sweetest utterance to have ever left his lips, or at least one of them. Who knew this big burly beast of a man with a scowl that could injure an opponent at ten paces, could be so damn romantic.

Every cell in my body is vibrating, the realisation that we are really all alone finally hitting me. My brain is a tizzy with all the things I could do to this man without being interrupted. I rise on my tiptoes and press my lips against his, softly at first, but it isn't enough for my Soldier boy. Gripping onto my hips he pulls me up so I can wrap my legs around his waist, and then he kisses me, like I am the life force that keeps his heart beating in his chest. Being suspended in his arms is quickly becoming my haven. Tongues lapping together between nips of his teeth against my lips, kissing Logan might just be my new favourite thing, well that and the indescribable orgasms he gifts me. Settling me on my feet he lets me loose, pointing me towards the sofa and slapping my arse before returning to what he was doing behind the kitchen island.

As though on cue my phone chimes with two notifications in quick succession and I swipe at the screen to open the message thread.

Merry Christmas Babe. Me, Randy and the boys are at mum and dad's, Logan has a strict forty-eight hour no return policy set in place, so I look forward to seeing you both on Tuesday. Mum is baking like she's about ready to feed the five thousand so expect to binge on a fuck tonne of carbs when you get here.

I love that you are both finally admitting your feelings but feel free to keep what happens in the cabin for the next two days to yourselves.

In this instance, sharing is not caring.

Have fun!

Candice xxx

Forty-eight hours of uninterrupted Logan appreciation, Merry fucking Christmas to me.

'For you,' he states, passing me my gift, encouraging me to open it with a nod of his head when I hesitate. I reach out and stroke the bow tie tight across his bulging Adams apple and that touch alone has goosebumps prickling my skin. For the briefest of moments, I get lost in the intensity of his gaze, a slave to his next word as I grip the gift between my fingers.

A master of distraction - another attribute to add to the list of Logan.

I sit on the edge of the sofa and rest the box on my knees, toying with the note and glancing up at him, realising now he had ordered this for me before anything had happened between us. This wasn't a one off, he hadn't lied when he had told me he had wanted me before this weekend.

Carefully untying the organza bow I remove the lid and paw through the expensive sheets of red packing paper embossed with a glittery snowflake design. I laugh heartily when I find my very own pair of rabbit ears attached to a red velvet Santa hat with a fluffy white trim. An unexpected tear teeters on my lash line as my chest warms with his sweet sentiment, I realise I had never given Logan the chance to be this way with me, I had been so blinded by my misplaced rage I had missed out on having this with him for all this time. Whether or not I had thought I deserved him, the fact is I wanted him, and that should have been enough.

'You don't like it?' He worries, misreading my tear-filled eyes for sadness.

'I love it, who knew Logan Sinclair was such a talented gift giver.'

'Orgasms and outfits, that's probably as far as that particular talent reaches. And both of those I get to enjoy while I'm buried to the hilt inside you. Feels like a win win sort of situation,'

'Two of my favourite things,' I chuckle, pulling out my messy top knot and letting my unruly red waves fall down around my shoulders, tugging the hat down onto my head and making sure the ears are standing to attention.

Beneath the hat is a ruby red lace corset, a matching pair of booty shorts and a pair of candy cane stripped stockings with white fur trims. Holding up the structured bodice, I admire the beautiful detailing of the garment, running my fingers over the delicate stitching of my nickname sewn into the fabric under the edging of sweetheart neckline. I look to Logan for an explanation, knowing that he had no idea I would be here this Christmas so he couldn't have ordered this outfit with the personalisation in the short time frame. All I'm met with is a boyish grin.

'I knew how much you regretted your costume at my birthday party, how you wished you had worn an outfit more suited to your sexy, fiery nature. I wanted you to have that. I wanted you to see yourself how I see you. Not to say the fluffy pink number wasn't cute as fuck,' he beams. I had wanted desperately to feel like one of those women hanging off his body that night, believing until now that it was impossible.

I am lost in a stunned silence as I trace my finger over the brand on the corset again, trying to comprehend that even back then he thought of me as more than just his little sister's best friend.

'You stitched this yourself?' I ask, a little dumbfounded at his thoughtfulness.

I catch sight of Logan as he toys his lower lip between his fingers, a nervous energy radiating from him as he watches me admire the gift.

'Seems I'm not just a pretty face, not too shabby with a needle and thread either.' He adds nonchalantly, like this isn't the most thoughtful present I have ever received.

'Keep burrowing Little Bunny,' he grins, crossing his arms over his chest and gesturing with a nod towards the box on my lap.

'Well, well, well. Is there not a by-law that frowns upon the unauthorised use of official army equipment?' I tease, letting the silver metal handcuffs swing back and forth on my finger.

'I am a Lieutenant; I get special treatment.' He gruffly replies, hitting me with a roguish wink.

Jumping to my feet, still clutching the handcuffs, I run to him and press my lips against his, our tongues battling as I show my gratitude at his thoughtfulness.

When I pull away, my heart is thumping in my chest, his arms around my waist tightening, the outline of his impressive cock pressing against my belly through the rough fabric of his trousers.

'Floppy ears and a rock-hard erection look good on you Soldier Boy.'

'Oh, you ain't seen nothing yet Bunny. I have plans for you, none of which would be considered festive season appropriate,'

A girlish giggle bursts from my lips when he digs his fingers into the hollow of my hip, anticipation coating my skin with a light sheen of sweat, the roaring open fire colouring our joined bodies with a soft amber glow.

Who would have thought a six-foot-four Adonis with a sweet nature, and a sinfully dirty mouth, dressed as the personification of the fucking Easter bunny working a Magic Mike reunion, could make a girl so freaking wet. Niagara Falls has nothing on me right now.

CHAPTER *nineteen*

MIA

Freshening up, I change into the outfit Logan had so thoughtfully got me and apply a little red lipstick to finish off the look. With my red curls swept into a side parting and ruffled, the bunny ears and Santa hat set in place, I feel sexier than I ever have before. The candy cane stockings reach to mid-thigh and whilst I didn't think to even bring heels on this trip, I find an old pair of black stilettos in Candice's wardrobe that I had left here from our party days. They are a little battered and probably coated in dried tequila shots but nothing a little wipe over can't fix. I can't imagine with the way this corset is pushing up my boobs that Logan will even be looking at my feet. I switch out the booty shorts for a lacy red thong from my collection still tucked away in the top drawer of Logan's dresser and I think I'm about ready to head back downstairs. I refuse to let the nerves settle as I step into the living room where I left him, using them in place of the confidence this outfit should raise in me. Nursing two

thumbs of whiskey in a cut glass tumbler, I see the moment Logan's soul appears to leave his body, his eyes wide, his grin wider.

'Well fuck me sideways, Bunny. You look good enough to eat,' he states, knocking back the rest of his drink and licking his full lips, placing the glass down on the sofa's side table and getting to his feet. Even though I'm wearing high heels, he still seems to tower over me. He runs his finger across my exposed collarbone, barely making contact with my skin, but the ghost of his touch is enough to have me stumbling forward into him, to solidify the connection. If the past two days have taught me anything, it's that I will probably be forever greedy for more of him.

Placing both palms on his bare tattooed chest I guide him back until he falls down onto the sofa. He doesn't complain, he also doesn't let go of my hips and I fall down with him, straddling his thighs and wriggling in his lap until I'm comfy.

'Do you want your present, Sir?' I coo, using the last brain cells not completely obliterated by this man's touch, while performing the question with a suggestive flick of my hips. He quirks a brow, knowing I would have had to be inventive with something that already existed in this house, considering we've snowed in. He nods gingerly as he fingers the fluffy tops of my stockings appreciatively and I plant a kiss on his cheek, leaving a smudged red lipstick print on his skin.

I linger there, close enough to his ear to lick it, and say, 'How about an extra special one-of-a-kind visual aid.' I don't give him time to work out what I'm proposing when I press the button on the video splice app on my phone. Our home video of last night's extra-curricular activities in Logan's bedroom plays out on the big surround sound screen on the wall to our left, via the Bluetooth link. Between power naps and all the rigorous sex, I had found some time in the early hours of this morning to put it all together. Sure, it wasn't a flashy gift, or as heartfelt as his matching bunny costumes, but if his smile is anything to go by, he loves it. His cock hardens beneath me as he watches the birds eye view of me taking him into my mouth, gagging a little as he hits the back of my throat, even with that I can't fit him all in, but I certainly gave it my best. He groans and shifts beneath me, his brutal grip on my hips tightening when he repeatedly rocks me back and forth over his lap, his cock digging up into my core. His hand runs up the length of my spine, even through the fabric of my bustier I can feel the connection against my sensitive skin. I arch into the touch, always needy for more of whatever he is offering. When he reaches the base of my neck his fingers descend into my mane of red unruly curls, grabbing a handful and forcing my face forward, my nose skimming his as our breaths mingle.

'What do you say Bunny, fancy playing a game?' He grins, swallowing the whimper ready to fall from my lips when he holds me tight against his body and hits me with a bruising kiss.

CHAPTER Twenty

MIA

'Tie me up, strap me down, chase me for an eternity, I'm ready to be owned every which way you deem fit Mr. Floppy.' I assert as I reach up and stroke one of the furry bunny ears on his head, giddy at the prospect of him taking everything he wants from my body.

'I'll have you know there is nothing floppy about me right now,' He grins, rolling me over his tenting length to second his point. Lifting me as he stands, my thighs tighten around his waist as he crosses the room with me in his arms and lowers me down onto the kitchen island, the grey marble cold against my heated skin.

'I think a safe word is in order,' he adds, filling the space between my parted thighs as he traces the sweetheart neckline of my outfit that is struggling to contain my ample cleavage. With the way he is looking at me right now, I can appreciate the pros of owning more underwear like this. Tapping his bare foot on the floorboards he waits for me to propose a safe word that I know will never leave my lips while he is worshipping me, his patience wanes, the sounds of us fucking on the TV pushing him to new levels that have his fingers twitching. Taunting Logan right now, when all he wants to do is throw me down against any available surface and thrust up inside me, shouldn't be turning me on as much as it is. Having Logan around me, on me and in me is literally the holy grail trifecta and there is nothing I wouldn't do for him, but toying with him, that never gets old, our very own aphrodisiac that has been put on hold for the past three years. At this point we're playing catch up.

'Safe word Bunny, don't make me ask you again.' He retorts sternly, the commanding Lieutenant in him breaking through the surface and interrupting my train of thought. His dipped gaze is filled with an authority that promises dark and wonderful things. His whole demeanour has shifted, and it obliterates the cute playfulness of the bunny ears and bowtie combo he's still wearing.

'Candy cane,' I softly mewl, pressing my lips against his ever so lightly, a teasing touch that has his cock jumping in his jeans. Smiling at me I notice the wash of confidence in his expression, as though he's calling my bluff to whatever thought I am having that has me appearing so confident. A feral glint of need glazes over his muddy green gaze, burning embers of carnal desire flickering in the depths. I can see the makings of an idea bloom on his face, his features taking on a curious edge as he steps towards the Christmas tree, removing two lengths of tinsel and running them through his fingers.

'Technically, that is two words Bunny, I asked for one.' He chuckles but it lacks all humour, as he winds one end of the two strands of tinsel around his meaty fist, as though he is silently weighing up options I'm not privy to.

My core flutters with approval at what should be considered an innocent move, but I can tell by the twisted grin on his face that nothing from here on out will be anything but purposeful. Selecting a song on his phone he crosses the room towards me as *Eartha Kitt's 'Santa Baby'* begins to play out of the speakers and I can't stifle the warm bubble of laughter that rumbles out of me.

'How fitting,' I say cockily, wetting my lips, my mouth bone dry. The song I had replayed in my head a million times since that day in the treehouse, when I had asked Logan to be my first kiss, feels different somehow. With us like this, exploring a new and wondrous facet of whatever it is that we are now, I thank the twist of fate that had led me home early from work that night to find Trevor face deep between another woman's legs. This man right here, is mine, of that I'm sure, the truth is he has had me heart, body and soul ever since that day in the treehouse. He lifts one length of tinsel over my head, so it falls down over my shoulders, so I'm wearing it like a scarf. Yet another splash of festive whimsy to add to my outfit. Trailing his finger down my arm he wordlessly commands my attention, his tongue darting out to wet his lips as he lifts me from the side and plants me on my feet. My hands go behind to brace myself against the side as he eats up the space between our bodies, effectively caging me in.

'I may not have had your first,' he begins, clearly remembering that day like I had, as our song plays out of the speaker. 'I may not have had your first,' he repeats. 'But I want all of your lasts Bunny. I want to worship every inch of this beautiful body until you are begging me to stop.' He says softly, bending so his lips can trail down my neck, his warm whiskey-soaked breath tickling my pulse point. Always two steps ahead of me his words act as a distraction. When I move to affectionately cup his face, to run my palm across the dusting of stubble across his jaw, I find I can't move my arms. Pinned behind my back the tinsel rustles as I attempt to tug my wrists apart, the irony of it making Logan chuckle with pride as the similar jostling sound of sleighs on snow chime in the backing track of the song. He takes a step back and I watch with interest as he begins to slowly undo his belt, my knees threatening to give way as I sway on the spot, the throbbing between my thighs almost too much.

'Logan, please,' I beg, unashamed at how much I need this man.

'I asked for *A* safe word,' He grumbles, emphasis on the A, his voice like liquid gold running over every inch of my exposed skin. I knew I'd pay for that infraction eventually.

'Fuck' I squeak.

'That one won't do Bunny, I plan on making you say that particular word a hell of a lot. Now turn around and bend over the edge of the sofa,' he orders, snapping the two lengths of leather together so a whipping sound permeates the air, the noise of it an almost tangible entity that licks at my flesh. I do as he has instructed and get in place.

129

'Bite down on this,' he orders, slipping the length of a large candy cane between my lips, my teeth bared around it as the sweet sugary coating settles on my tongue. Trailing a finger down the length of my spine I feel him retreat, that familiar shuffling of his jeans being pushed down his legs. I crane my neck back to get a look but the harsh stripe of the belt against my arse cheek stills me.

'No peeking Bunny.' He orders gruffly, stepping forward, using his free hand to untie and release the silk ribbon slotted through the clasps lining the back of my bodice with ease. I groan around the candy cane in my mouth, my spine arching as the addictive mixture of pleasure and pain that rocketed through my lower half at the contact of his belt, continues to sizzle through my extremities. My breathing quickens, the angle of my body slumped over the sofa making my calf muscles uncomfortably taut. I wriggle a little on the spot and that earns me another biting slap to the other cheek with the belt. My arousal spikes up another two notches, any more of this and I know I will find my release, and he's barely even touched me.

Pinching my clit between his fingers he pulls aside my lacy thong and thrusts up inside me without warning, I'm already slick enough that it only takes a moment or two for my core to comfortably accept his sizeable length. I shudder around the overwhelming fullness as white spots dance behind my eyes. I feel the length of tinsel graze against my skin as Logan readjusts its position against my throat, that delicious burn of pressure when he effectively leashes me, controlling my body as he tugs on it to check that I'm okay with it.

'More' Is the only muffled word I can get out around the candy cane still clenched between my teeth and it clearly does the job, when Logan winds the lengths of tinsel hanging over each shoulder down my back around his white knuckled fist. Bottoming out he rolls his hips whilst buried to the hilt, his fingers tightening on my hip as he licks a path up my spine, his body folding to mould to my back. Lifting me in one fluid motion he rests my knees on the edge of the sofa. His hand tugging at the tinsel looped around my neck so my head falls back onto his shoulder, the other working me up as he rubs in circular motions against my sensitive bud of nerves. I flatten my hands between our bodies as best as I can, as my palms rest against his stomach, the tinsel wound around my wrists pinching at my flesh. It doesn't take long, and I sail over the precipice, my body thrumming as goosebumps skitter across my bare skin. With two more thrusts, the dizzying pressure of the tinsel constricting my breathing, I'm lightheaded as another orgasm rockets through me, Logan chasing his own release a moment later with a guttural roar of 'MINE' as he tips his head back and stakes his claim of me to the heavens.

Going limp in his arms, his heart beating frantically in his chest against my back. We don't move, enjoying the last remnants of our collective bliss as he slowly pulls out of me. The waning fissure of an insatiable hunger rumbling just beneath the surface of my skin.

The candy cane falls to the floor as my slack jaw releases it, the crumbling sweet coating splintering on impact thanks to the assault it endured between my clenched teeth. I inhale and exhale in heavy splutters. He unwinds one of the loops of the tinsel enough that I can get one hand free, the rest of it still attached to the other wrist. Turning me to face him, kneading my upper arms as a form of aftercare, he comes down from his own high, laying a chaste kiss on my trembling lips. I take this moment of calm to catch him off guard and surprise him, I lunge at him, and jump into his arms as he staggers back, the back of his legs hitting the edge of the sofa. Falling down to sit I roll my hips as I straddle him. I dot featherlight nips and kisses against his throat, as his head falls back, opening his neck up for more attention. I wind the length of tinsel he untied to free my hand around his wrist, so we're tethered together, I use my teeth to secure the knot. I know he could snap it in two and free himself with very little effort, but the lust swimming in his muddy green eyes tells me he won't.

'Round two Mr. Not-so-Floppy?' I question, already knowing the answer as his cock begins to harden beneath me. Using the metal chain of his dog tags I pull him in close, kissing him hungrily as I happily drown in the dream that I had for so long hoped would come true. Being here, with him, losing ourselves in this new version of us, I feel complete.

'Any last words?' I ask him, running my thumb over his lower lip stained with my lipstick.

'You are the best gift I could ever get, epic homemade porn a very close second. I will be grateful every day I get to call you mine and I promise to make up for the last three years that I wasn't where I should have been, buried inside you at every possible opportunity. I should have told you how I felt that night, I should have demanded and pleaded with you to listen. This is how it was always meant to be

Bunny, tied together, and lost in each other's orbits, hopping through life side by side.' He smiles broadly, dimples on show, repositioning my bunny ears on my head and pulling me in closer, so there is only a sliver of space between our bodies.

'I'll hop along beside you for however long you'll have me, Soldier Boy.' I say lovingly running his dog tags through my fingers, meaning every word as my heart swells in my chest. Pulling his face to meet mine I kiss him fiercely, with everything I have, because right now, we don't need any more words.

As Christmas miracles go, this is one for the books, all we needed was a little bit of snow, a fuck-tonne of festive magic, and a long-lost memory of young love in its purest form...

Oh, and his cock, forgetting to add his magnificent cock to my little list would be a travesty....

Thank you so much for reading Logan & Mia's story, I hope you enjoyed it. If you would be happy to leave a review for *'His Christmas Bunny'* on Amazon, Goodreads, bookbub and anywhere else you can think of it would be greatly appreciated. If you enjoyed it, spreading the word and recommending this book really helps also…. Keep a look out via my socials or newsletter for a bonus epilogue coming soon.

I hope you have a Merry Christmas filled with plenty more smutty festive reads.
If you are looking to add some more books to your TBR
'VERONICA' and 'OLIVIA' - Dual POV standalone reads in the Twisted Fates series,
are available online and in Kindle Unlimited.

To get up to date news, first pick of future ARCS, snippets & giveaways please join up to my newsletter.

If you would like to be a part of my hype street team on Facebook & help spread the word about my books, I would love to have you on board, there will be exclusives & freebies at Billie Jade Kermack's hype & street team

I also have a FB group where we chat about all things romance and books & all are welcome at Billie Jade Kermack Romance Reader Group

This QR code leads to everything you need to find me and my books

Mrs. Floppy Sinclair

My Logan List

Thong stealer

Master of distraction

Tinsel play genius

A literal God

Good with his hands

Cute as Hell

Magnificent Cock

Soldier Boy ♥ His Bunny

'OLIVIA' SNEAK PEEK

OUT NOW IN EBOOK, PAPERBACK & KU

Chapter One

Well spank my arse and call me Candy. When did sending flowers go out of fashion?' My friend Sophie splutters as she places a fresh Gin and Tonic down onto the battered wooden table in front of me. 'Olivia, you have me questioning your state of mind,' she clucks, her wide brown eyes glued to my mobile. Using my given first name where she would usually shorten it to *livvie*, she adopts a disapproving motherly tone. Her slick grin and the glint of mirth in her widened gaze says otherwise though. She is desperate for information.

The bar is flooded with light, every surface painted with varying shades of honey gold, as the late afternoon sun streams in through the floor to ceiling wraparound shop front. The words scrawled on the oversized specials board above the bar glitter, as wafts of steam from the coffee machines below disturb my view.

Situated in the heart of London, *Taylor's* is the go-to location, the eclectic melting pot of patrons from varying trades and standing keeping it interesting for someone like me, who lives to people watch. It's not every day you see a woman dressed head to toe in fur; an outfit I'm sure cost more than my flats extortionate rent and then some, as she nibbles at her breakfast pastry, holding a chunk between her teeth and dipping to feed it to her sausage dog Walter, like he's a baby bird. The edge of disgust creeping across my features at the sight, is immediately chased away when she turns and catches me staring, I hit her with a megawatt smile and a nod of my head in greeting, as I silently celebrate her eccentricities. Maude, and others like her, while often strange in their ways, are what make *Taylor's* so great. Maude is as ingrained in the bones of this place as is the *'Johnny's mum loves cock,'* graffiti, that had been crudely carved into the bathroom stall door, on the day Travis opened the bar to the public.

The unseasonably warm weather, which doesn't seem to be affecting Maude as she looks prepared to battle an Antarctic winter, leaves the scent of suncream hanging in the air as customers flood through the now propped open doors. I almost miss the whimsical tinkering of the bell that chimes when someone new enters when the winds outside are bitter, and this place is their haven to escape the elements. Today is particularly busy for a Tuesday and Sophie should be working, but with an encouraging nudge of my elbow I realise she hasn't had her fill of my love life dramas just yet. Tugging at her red tabard apron that compliments the matching table runners throughout the bar, Sophie releases the top button of her white work shirt, as she adjusts herself in the seat beside me to get comfortable. I continue to scroll through the photos now that she's invested, listening for the squeaks of shock that rumble from her lips when a new one loads. The roulette wheel of what to expect ranging from a guy holding up a prize-winning fish wearing chest waders,

to a guy posing naked on black sheeting meant for a very different type of water sports, the latter, of the golden shower variety.

'What the fuck?' She adds as she moves in a little closer to get a better look at the photo currently lighting up my screen, the ends of her sharp blonde bob tickling my cheek.

'My sentiments exactly.' I chuckle swiping my raven curls back over my shoulder. Fanning my cheeks as she inspects the image with pinched brows. Moving to one side, I pull a grip from my pocket and pin the bleached strands of hair that usually frame my face, up into a fifties inspired quiff atop my head, grateful for the splash of cool air against my face. I like the warm weather as much as the next person, but sweaty boobs, that's where I draw the line.

'Sorry. But Christ, is that meant to bend that way?' She asks, her inquisitiveness causing one of her brows to rise as she pulls my attention back to the screen.

We both tilt our heads to the left slowly, a synchronised move as though they are being manipulated by a string, our jaws slack and brows pinched as I struggle with the urge to swipe across the screen and zoom in on the picture. The half-naked *gentleman*, who I am pretty sure isn't really a gentleman at all, is staring up at us with a devilish grin plastered over his stubbled face looking like a pure blood Nordic God with his sharp jaw, straight nose, blonde hair and bright blue eyes. I now know him simply as BigGlen29 from Bristol. The ruler he is holding in the hand not secured around the base of his cock, leaves nothing to the imagination and although confidence is always a bonus, the unsolicited Dick Pics never really screamed life-long romance for me. It's murky waters trying to stay afloat on dating apps these days. You could apply a Dr. Suess poem for the number of cocks I've been introduced to since joining up to *Sally's Soulmates*.

One cock, two cock, maybe eight, Soft cock, long cock, ooh a thick one, Great! Even the little voice in my head has an edge of sarcasm to it.

'Get your fill honey, this is the third one I've received today, and at least BigGlen29 had the forethought to tend to a little manscaping before he sent over his naked submission, RandyBob69 was giving off Chewbacca vibes.' I say scrunching up my nose in distaste. Not satisfied with the mere impression I might be leaving her with I swipe through my messages and pull up the photo I had received over breakfast that caused me to paint the kitchen worktop with my morning sweet tea.

'Well at least you'd never get cold, you could hibernate in that chest hair,' she chuckles, squinting to see the tattooed skin beneath.

Her face contorts and I can't hold back the bark of laughter rumbling up my throat as she grimaces. Unable to tear her gaze away from the screen as she tries to make sense of what she is looking at I continue with my little slide show, stopping when she gasps and dips down for a better look. I'm familiar with the odd sense of intrigue that has her eyes wide, and her jaw relaxed with surprise, that sort of car crash appeal that steals away every modicum of your attention.

'Well,' she chortles, almost choking on the word as she tries to catch her breath, 'he certainly doesn't need a ruler, that is what us single ladies refer to as a beast of a man.' She sucks in a rush of air, clenching her thighs as the torso of an Asian man with a ripped moulded chest whose face is out of focus fills my screen.

'In more ways than one.' I offer. I watch her splay her palm out in the air between us, gripping around an imaginary cock to gauge how big KingCobra22 might be in real life. Now even though

I know proportions can be manipulated online, and that there is every chance KingCobra22 is in fact a fifty-two-year-old man, still living in his mother's basement with a remote job as a telemarketer, I decide to keep my thoughts to myself, because I like the giddy glint of excitement pinching at her cheeks right now. I like to live vicariously through my friend, I'd give anything to see the world how she does, with passion and awe, her cup never half full but rather always brimming over. I never actually meet with any of the guys on this app, downloading it was for research purposes only, and I know that sounds like something some dick hungry girl would say, but in this instance it's true. I want to be that girl that thinks she is the one in a million against the odds that finds true love on the internet, but the universe isn't exactly swinging the prince charming's my way. My recent foray into becoming a writer has been harder than I first thought it would be. Apparently having a talent to write well has zero to do with the politics of getting into the world of publishing. With my eighth rejection email idly waiting to be printed and pinned up on my wall, it's yet another notch carved out of my willpower to continue searching for a literary agent. Clearly a glutton for punishment, I decide to drown my sorrows with another gulp of my drink.

Alcohol, that's the way to go, numb the pain, Olivia. I welcome the thought and swallow the pain lodged in my throat with a mouthful of crisp British bred Gin, or mother's ruin as my father so often referred to it. It had in fact ruined my own mother at most family occasions when I was growing up, so he had a point and the evidence in the family photo albums that I couldn't refute. I didn't much mind my mother addled due to booze, it meant she wasn't concentrating on how I had royally disappointed her that day.

With the booming clang of a bell hung above the bar Travis signals the waitresses to the next round of drinks ready for table service, and although this is clearly my friend's job and the bar is packed with people, she ignores him and slinks a little further down into the seat beside me, as though he hasn't already seen her, rolling her wrist, urging me to show her the other candidates' photos. I don't know exactly what these guys are applying for, but it kept it somewhat professional to call them candidates. The fact that some of them would find themselves as muse material for characters in the many manuscripts I am currently working on is beside the point. Sophie leans in to take a sip of my drink as she mentally prepares herself for the guys who think it's perfectly acceptable to greet a stranger on the internet with a 4k viewing of their nether regions. I feel like *Sally's swingers* would be a more apt business name for this particular dating website.

'How do you respond to these?' She chuckles, a glint of genuine curiosity darkening her coppery brown irises.

'With a smile and copious amounts of alcohol.' I respond flatly, holding up my glass. Sophie missed the memo about online dating, contentedly grazing through life with what I would call a prince charming to do list. It was rare that the odd guy she might find attractive and interesting in the bar she would allow into her bed, and those she did were generally a solid eight out of ten with a three-date minimum as experience. But my friend has a vision, and not one of those fairy-tale chance meetings started with her trolling the internet for possible cock encounters. Her phone is filled with Pinterest boards of new home décor, and one pot wonders perfect for those cold Autumn evenings, mine are filled with smutty book recs with half naked alphas on the covers and coupons for discounted wine crates. We are not the same.

'How do you get them to go away? I can't imagine guys that are willing to send this via a messaging service are quick to take no for an answer.'

'I google images of dicks, a little cropping and some photo enhancing I then return the favour, freaks them out and they block me, saves me from all the hassle of trying to avoid them.'

'You are a genius,' she giddily chimes in, still swiping at my screen because apparently her piqued interest is currently overriding her usual need to warn me of the dangers of such a site.

'Let's just hope no-one pulls up my search history, the rabbit hole of insane shit people put out into the world is not for the faint of heart,' I quip. Kinky doesn't come close to describing what some people do for pleasure. I'd never yuck someone's yum but even I have my limits. Sophies eyes light up, a flicker of excitement rimming her darkened brown irises with a searing amber. Sophie likes sex as much as the next girl, she just prefers her men with a little more decorum. These guys are nice to look at, sure, but they would never make it past the first date with her, even for research purposes.

'So, is this what you do when you're procrastinating, weeding out unsuitable matches online?' She queries, chewing on the inside of her cheek as she tries to gauge just how dangerous my extracurricular activities online might be. She knows how lost I've been of late, and I know she cares, but she is quick to hide her concern, knowing I refuse to entertain any form of sympathy from her.

'What can I say, being a romance author has its ups and downs. The book isn't exactly panning out right now.' I huff, that

flicker of hope that clarity and a bestselling idea will just magically hit me.

'You know you have to actually spend time at your laptop to get the words in there, right?' Soph adds.

'I'm lacking the required inspiration right now. Love can only be prettied up with fancy words and relatable scenes when the author isn't wallowing in self-pity and crippling sadness.' I bite back with zero bark. I know she's right. She doesn't answer me this time, instead she wisely edges the glass of alcohol closer to me, staying far enough away to dodge my sorrow like it's a spreadable disease.

'It seems like a take your vitamins with a glass of wine sort of day,' Soph says, rubbing little circles into my back as though I need consoling.

'You're not wrong there. I'll make a note to add that to my next order,' I mumble as I neck the entire offered glass of crisp refreshing liquid. I get to my feet, catching Travis' gaze as he fills an order. He's too far away to hear me but must sense my question just by the look on my face. I crudely mime the shape of a wine bottle this time as the Gin just isn't cutting it. Charades is clearly not my thing because it takes him a minute or so, after holding up various bottles of alcohol to finally hold up a fruity Australian 2019 Sauvignon Blanc. I shoot him a thumbs up, the universal sign of acceptance that thankfully doesn't need any further explanation. Travis and I went to college together, when I was flouncing around doing ballet, he was applying himself in advanced business classes. Travis Taylor is up and coming, and already planning to open his next bar up North. Another server delivers the wine to the table and Sophie promptly tops up the fresh glass beside it. I note that Travis has only sent over one

glass, a sign to remind Sophie that she's meant to be working, but it fails to do as intended as she continues to rest her elbow against the crudely carved wooden tabletop, her fist propping up her chin as she stares at me.

'Distract me Soph, inspire me. How's your love life coming along. Feel free to be descriptive.' I press, needing a respite from my own life right now.

'I'm in desperate need to get taken out; suitor or sniper, I'm not fussy at this point, it's been one of those weeks,' she harrumphs sulkily as I giggle around the rim of my glass. Leave it to my best friend to lighten the mood.

'You heard anything more from Dillon?' As I ask the question, I watch her face screw up, clear revulsion marring her features for the path our conversation has taken. Not her usual eight out of ten on the hot guy scale then.

'God no, thank fuck. Barely even given him a second thought.'

'Barely?' I ask with a grin plastered on my face, suspicious that it is the one word she lingered on.

'I got a little too rigorous with brushing my teeth the other day, practically assaulted my gag reflex. Sometimes I can't help but think of him.'

'Is that your roundabout way of telling me Dillon was hung like a donkey?' I add.

'Yes. Sadly, he was also donkey-brained, you simply can't train stupid, no matter how well acquainted they get with your cervix,' she sighs, crossing her legs beneath the table as the statement has her body reacting to a memory of him.

'VERONICA' SNEAK PEEK

OUT NOW IN EBOOK, PAPERBACK & KU

Only suitable for 18+ due to the nature of the contents.

TRIGGER WARNINGS

Rape

SA

Abortion

Descriptive sex scenes

Vulgar speech

Drink and drug use

Chapter One

RONI

Fck you, fuck whatever this is, and for sure, fuck that!' I spit, lingering on the word *that* as my lip curls up in disgust. My eyes fix on the woman with her legs draped around my boyfriend's waist. I scan around the flat that I had called *home* for the past two years, but the space suddenly feels foreign to me. The bag of greasy fast-food goodies in my hand falls towards the floor; lettuce and cola exploding out onto my battered *Converse* as I try to comprehend the sight before me.

'He already did,' the woman I'll forever refer to as *that* replies cockily with a slick smile that lasts for all of 1.3 seconds. Realising her mistake, she swallows back her confidence as her grin fades, arranging the bed

runner that I had purchased around herself so less of her peachy skin is on show. She shrinks back behind my boyfriend's still heavy breathing form like the coward she is, and I gulp in air to steady myself. Little does she know that if I wanted to, not even this gelatinous excuse for a man could stop me from rearranging her build-a-bear-painted face. Who knew Hashtag Whore Barbie was trending for Christmas? The cheap ruby red lipstick smeared across her Botox-infused lips and up his bearded neck makes me shudder. I attempt to make sense of the ungodly episode of animal kingdom that has been playing out in front of me since I entered the flat. But the grunting and uncoordinated slapping of skin I'd silently witnessed before finding my voice only proves to embed the unwanted visuals further into my brain. Is it too much to hope for spontaneous human combustion?

'We love each other,' the gutless bitch snipes, a poor attempt to fill the uncomfortable silence. Her voice breaks before she can finish the sentence.

'Calm down *"Debbie Does Dalston"*, the grown-ups are talking,' I retort sardonically, my feet still glued to the spot. I want nothing more than to run away, but my need to dominate the situation and not appear weak has me tethered in place. I make a mental note to thank my mother for my tenacity; it's a trait we share.

'Jealous much?' *That* smirks, running her bubble-gum pink manicured fingers down my boyfriend's torso. He wisely moves to push her hand away as bile rises in my throat. The sneaky portion of mozzarella sticks I had wolfed down in the car ride over threatening to make an appearance.

'In order for me to be jealous of you, Morgan, it would require that you have something I want. Right now, you are merely helping me shed some dead weight,' I bite back sarcastically as I fight to centre my wayward emotions that threaten to overwhelm my thoughts. I glance up at the mirrored ceiling above us as though viewing the situation

from another angle would make it any less horrific. I shake my head to dispel thoughts of them together; what I'd seen from the door had been enough to make me lose my appetite for good.

Watching her wind her finger around the pole-straight blonde extensions framing her face, I note how different we are. My low-maintenance chocolate waves are thrown into a messy bun; my face is without a lick of makeup; remnants of ketchup stain the oversized hoodie I've worn for two days straight. I'm chalk to her cheese.

What had I done to deserve such a crappy boyfriend and an equally crappy sister? My list of things to accomplish before turning thirty has quickly morphed from an episode of *Happy Days* into a rerun of *Luther*. All I have now is a depressing list of my failures and how royally I've fucked up my life by trusting such utter cockwombles.

'Well, Merry-fucking-Christmas to me,' I say lightly, although the tears in my eyes deceive my resolve. I may not be jealous of Morgan, but I

am certainly hurt by her decision to betray me. Out of the two of them, her lack of loyalty cuts me the deepest. 'Who knew you had such sticky fingers, Morgan? I didn't know that sharing my toys was still an issue for you,' I press through gritted teeth, running my glare over the man I thought I would spend my forever with.

'Sharing is caring,' Morgan replies thoughtlessly with a sickly-sweet grin. I tear the engagement ring off my finger and throw it at them. My sister, ever the opportunistic princess, grabs for it and scrutinises the stone with beady eyes.

'It's fake. You'll probably get all of £3.50 from it, not even enough to get those pretty lips touched up,' I note, as she palms the worthless piece of metal anyways, just as I knew she would. Morgan has never cared about such simplicities as allegiance and consideration; she's always been fuelled by money and status. Before this moment, they

were traits that made her seem quite innocent and naïve. Although looking at her now, I know without a shadow of a doubt, that this bitch

knew exactly what she wanted. She knew how to get it, and she didn't care who she had to stomp on to get herself there.

'Roni, you don't understand,' Marcus states, finally joining the conversation, continuing to stay seated on the edge of the bed rather than approach me. I wouldn't be held responsible for what level of *Rocky Balboa* I'd channel when re-arranging his face if he continued to push me.

'Oh no, you don't understand,' I correct him. Stumbling forward, my feet finally obey my brain's instructions to move, and thankfully, I don't fall. 'One day, you are going to look back on this moment and realise what a mistake you've made. I, however, will look back on it fondly. FREEDOM!' I yell, throwing my fisted hand up into the air, all *John Hughesy,* as I make my way over to the wardrobe. I pull out my gym bag, which is practically brand new, as my intentions to attend the gym only lasted for about a week into the new year. I shove my belongings

haphazardly into it, making a point to take both iPhone cables just to piss him off. I zone out their heated whispers and continue to pack, purposefully knocking some breakables onto the floor as I go. The petty satisfaction as Marcus flinches and reacts is the only thing that helps me banish my tears.

With scorn fuelling me, I grab a thick black sharpie from his desk and pop off the lid, eyeing my ex- fiancé menacingly. A small smile curves at the corners of my lips as he waits with bated breath for my next move. Our eyes lock as I move to scribble a large penis on the blank white wall behind me, a wall that we've watched a thousand movies on with his projector. I owe my ability to draw such a large rendition of the male genitalia, without glancing at my canvas once, to my best friend Aiden, one of the many talents he has shown me over the years. Still grasping the marker in my tensed-up fist, I make my way across the room. As I

reach the chest of drawers, Marcus's eyes widen with fear. Another thing that Aiden has taught me springs to mind.

With a steadying breath, I let the hate filling my body seep out of me like oil dancing across water as I knock the glass trophy signed by *Christiano Ronaldo*, Marcus' most prized possession, to the ground with the tip of the marker. The biting ache of anger-filled waves that swim in my belly dissipate; only calm, soft swirls of smugness remain.

'Oopsie,' I say sweetly as he throws his hands to his head in disbelief. Sheer devastation colours his face a pale green. I extend my arm and animatedly drop the pen like a stand-up comedian would a mic.

Never leave angry. Aiden's words ring in my head. Again, I smile, not even bothering to watch the carnage unfold as Marcus falls to his knees, scooping the shards of glass up into his hands, his mouth agape with shock.

It may be spiteful; my behaviour is probably tacky at best, but it's most definitely necessary. In those brief moments of hate-filled destruction of property, I regain my power and am now level-headed

enough to leave the flat with an amused smile tickling at the corners of my lips. Going all *Banksy* on his walls, all the rebellion with zero of the talent, I finish my splurge of graffiti madness with the scrawled italicised phrase, *Adios Bitches.*

I make my way to the front door with my filled bag hauled up over my shoulder and one arm laden with anything of value I could grab in my hurry to leave. With the palm of my free hand, I grasp the handle and turn on my heels to take one last look at the studio apartment where I had spent my last two years, suddenly accepting the swift change in direction my life is taking.

With despair as my only ally, I finally allow myself to accept the quiet modicum of calm that is desperate to shock my heart back to life. I don't initially recognise the sense of peace filling me, the *drip drip* of

realisation leading me to understand without question now, that my future has far more to offer me than my past ever did.

They don't deserve any more of my time or attention.

As I knew he would, Aiden accepts me with open arms; a glass of wine in one hand and a plate piled high with ketchup-smothered bacon sandwiches in the other; my best friend knows me well.

Printed in Great Britain
by Amazon